THE VINLAND SAGAS

ADVISORY EDITOR: BETTY RADICE

MAGNUS MAGNUSSON is an Icelander who has been resident in Scotland for most of his life. After a career in newspaper journalism in Scotland, he is now a freelance author and broadcaster, best known as the presenter of the BBC quiz programme 'Mastermind'. He is also Chairman of the Scottish Natural Heritage. He studied English and Old Icelandic at Oxford University, and his hobby is translating from Icelandic, both old and new. With Herman Pálsson he has translated three other Saga volumes for Penguin Classics; *Njal's Saga*, *King Harald's Saga* and *Laxdæla Saga*.

HERMANN PÁLSSON studied Icelandic at the University of Iceland and Celtic at University College, Dublin. He was formerly Professor in Icelandic at the University of Edinburgh, where he taught from 1950 to 1988. He is the General Editor of the New Saga Library and the author of many books on the history and literature of medieval Iceland: his more recent publications include *Legendary Fiction in Medieval Iceland* (with Paul Edwards), *Art and Ethics in Hrafnkel's Saga* and *Vikings in Russia* (with Paul Edwards). In addition to the three other Saga translations with Magnus Magnusson (*Njal's Saga*, *King Harald's Saga* and *Laxdæla Saga*), Hermann Pálsson has also translated *Hrafnkel's Saga* and (with Paul Edwards) *Egil's Saga*, *Orkneyinga Saga*, *Eyrbyggia Saga* and *Seven Viking Romances* for the Penguin Classics.

THE VINLAND SAGAS

The Norse Discovery of America

GRÆNLENDINGA SAGA
AND
EIRIK'S SAGA

TRANSLATED WITH AN INTRODUCTION BY
MAGNUS MAGNUSSON AND
HERMANN PÁLSSON

PENGUIN BOOKS

PENGUIN BOOKS

Published by the Penguin Group
Penguin Books Ltd, 80 Strand, London WC2R 0RL, England
Penguin Putnam Inc., 375 Hudson Street, New York, New York 10014, USA
Penguin Books Australia Ltd, 250 Camberwell Road, Camberwell, Victoria 3124, Australia
Penguin Books Canada Ltd, 10 Alcorn Avenue, Toronto, Ontario, Canada M4V 3B2
Penguin Books India (P) Ltd, 11 Community Centre, Panchsheel Park, New Delhi – 110 017, India
Penguin Books (NZ) Ltd, Cnr Rosedale and Airborne Roads, Albany, Auckland, New Zealand
Penguin Books (South Africa) (Pty) Ltd, 24 Sturdee Avenue, Rosebank 2196, South Africa

Penguin Books Ltd, Registered Offices: 80 Strand, London WC2R 0RL, England

www.penguin.com

This translation first published 1965
26

Copyright © Magnus Magnusson and Hermann Pàlsson, 1965
All rights reserved

Printed in England by Clays Ltd, St Ives plc
Set in Linotype Pilgrim

CONTENTS

INTRODUCTION

The two medieval Icelandic sagas translated in this volume tell one of the most fascinating stories in the history of exploration – the discovery and attempted colonization of America by Norsemen, five centuries before Christopher Columbus. In spare and vigorous prose they record Europe's first surprised glimpse of the eastern shores of the North American continent and the Native Americans who inhabited them.

The sagas describe how Eirik the Red, outlawed from Iceland late in the tenth century, founded an Icelandic colony on the western coast of Greenland; how a prudent young merchant named Bjarni Herjolfsson, hastening towards Greenland across the Denmark Strait in the wake of the first fleet of colonizers in 985 or 986, was blown blindly past his destination south-west across the Atlantic and there sighted unknown lands; and how some fifteen years later Leif the Lucky, son of Eirik the Red, bought the ship that had survived this voyage and steered it back to the shores of the New World to explore and if possible exploit Bjarni's chance discovery.

What Leif and his crew of thirty-five found there delighted them: wild grapes in profusion, rolling grasslands, vast stretches of towering timber, an abundance of game of all kinds, rivers teeming with giant salmon, meadows rich with a harvest of wild wheat, and a climate so kind that winter frosts were hardly known; even the dew seemed to them sweeter than anything they had ever tasted before. And Leif the Lucky, exulting in his find, named the country *Vínland*: 'Wineland', the land of grapes.

Other voyages of exploration followed, led by Leif's brothers. But the explorers now encountered natives whose appearance and habits indicate beyond doubt that they were Native Americans. These voyages of exploration culminated, according to the sagas, in the expedition led by a wealthy Icelandic merchant, Thorfinn Karlsefni, Leif's brother-in-law, whose second name means, appropriately, 'Makings of a man'. It was he who took the decisive step of attempting to found the first permanent European settlement in America.

These sagas have been a source of enormous controversy for the past century and more. No scholar doubts the authenticity of the central facts of exploration and colonization of the New World, but the accounts in the two sagas conflict with one another at several important points, and there has been endless argument about their relative merits as historical evidence, because the picture of early eleventh-century America they draw is tantalizingly hazy, a series of blurred impressions shot through with vivid details. On the evidence of the texts themselves, it has so far proved impossible to make irrefutable identifications of any of the particular bays and havens visited by the Norsemen, or of the exact location of their main settlement in Vinland. Various and ingenious calculations have been made on the basis of the somewhat equivocal navigational and topographical clues contained in the two sagas, and Vinland has been confidently located by enthusiasts in areas as far apart as Hudson Bay in the north and Virginia in the south. Every one of the theories put forward has had to disregard one or more inconsistencies between the two sagas or even within the sagas themselves; but, generally speaking, the most acceptable interpretation of the elusive information in the sagas suggests that Vinland (if it was anywhere) was in the New England region, and the majority of scholars have inclined to this view.

Until recently, archaeologists had failed to unearth any tangible evidence of the visits by the Norsemen which could lend support to any particular theory. Various alleged relics have turned up from time to time, but none of them has survived expert scrutiny, and many have been shown to be blatant forgeries.

In the 1960s, however, some very interesting discoveries were made in Newfoundland by Dr Helge Ingstad (former Governor of East Greenland and Spitzbergen) and his archaeologist wife. Basing his geographical calculations on the sailing times and directions given in the sagas and on a sixteenth-century Icelandic map of the North Atlantic drawn by Sigurdur Stefansson in 1590 (reproduced on p.121), he decided to explore Newfoundland as the likeliest location for Vinland. And at L'Anse aux Meadows, a bay in the north-east of the island, he came across sites which have now been conclusively identified as a Norse settlement dating from around the year 1000.

There are seven or eight dwelling-sites in this cluster, and a small smithy where Dr Ingstad found a stone anvil, several pounds of slag and pieces of bog-iron, some nails, and fragments of bronze. The houses seem to have been built to the Norse pattern, with walls of turf and wood, and one of them measures sixty feet by forty-five, comprising a large hall and four smaller rooms; the hall, like the Norse buildings excavated in Greenland, has an ember-hearth running down the centre. Dr Ingstad argued that bog-iron was unknown in the Stone-Age culture of the primitive Native Americans, and that the method by which this particular iron at the Newfoundland site was extracted is unmistakably Norse.

The site was re-excavated in the 1970s by an international team of archaeologists; Ingstad's identification was confirmed, and in 1978 it was designated as the first UNESCO World Heritage site, and Parks Canada erected a grandiose version of the presumed main building. But there is no proof that this particular site is the Vinland named by Leif the Lucky and Thorfinn Karlsefni. For one thing, it is inconsistent with the sagas at one crucial point – the grapes that gave Vinland its name; because wild grapes, it is believed, have never grown farther north than Passamaquoddy Bay, between Maine and New Brunswick. This automatically disqualifies Newfoundland as the location of Vinland, and no amount of philological juggling with the name (see footnote, p. 58) can wish this away. On the other hand, there may well have been several other expeditions from Greenland to the North American seaboard which these two sagas do not record, and it is by no means impossible that several settlements were attempted.

Dr Ingstad himself said that he thought it not unlikely that other sites might be discovered, even though he failed to come across any others during a careful 4,000-mile sea search of the littoral north from New England right into the Gulf of St Lawrence. Certainly, this discovery has done nothing to quench interest in the whole subject of these pre-Columban Norsemen in America. The Vinland Sagas have long been a battle-arena for hosts of scholars and enthusiasts intent on championing a cause or proving a conjecture, and no doubt the speculations will continue or even increase as a result of Dr Ingstad's discovery.

Already, more has been written about these Vinland Sagas than about any other Icelandic saga; but so much of it has been ill-informed or speculative that it has tended to stimulate scepticism about their real value.[1]

It is time that the sagas were once again allowed to speak for themselves. Too often they have been served up to the public in filleted versions, with their texts emended or cut or adapted or even conflated into a single uneasy narrative in an attempt to gloss over their inconsistencies. The sagas themselves have become obscured rather than illuminated by editors who arbitrarily selected textual variants to suit their own theories. In the mid twentieth century, research was done into the relationship between the two sagas and their manuscripts, and this enabled scholars to make some far-reaching reassessments. Many previous editions and translations can now be shown to have been based, partly at least, on discredited texts or mistaken assumptions; the purpose of this present volume is to provide a modern translation of the two sagas, entire and unabridged, in the context of this academic research, and to restore them to their proper position in the vast saga literature of medieval Iceland.

*

First of all it is essential to give them their historical perspective. It was no accident that the Vinland Sagas were written, nor that they were written each in its particular way; they grew nat-

1. For a complete bibliography on the Vinland Sagas and their problems, including the many previous translations into English, see *Islandica*, vols. I, II, XXIV, and XXXVIII, Cornell University Press, New York, 1908, 1909, 1935, and 1957.

urally out of the cultural and social conditions in Iceland in the twelfth and thirteenth centuries, as we shall see later. And in the same way, the historical event they commemorate – the discovery of Vinland by the Norsemen – was by no means so fortuitous as the first accidental sighting of it in 985 or 986 might suggest. There is an unbroken chain of inevitable progression between the discovery and subsequent settlement of, first, Iceland, then Greenland, and then Vinland. The discovery and attempted colonization of Vinland were the logical outcome of the great Scandinavian migrations that spilled over northern Europe in the early Middle Ages, the ultimate reach of the Norse surge to the west: it was on the Atlantic seaboard of North America that this huge impetus was finally exhausted.

The decisive moves towards the west were initiated by the Viking raiders of the last years of the eighth century. They came prowling across the North Sea in their longships and struck the first violent blows against the western kingdoms, hammer-blow assaults on the wealthy and undefended coastlines that earned them an imperishable reputation for viciousness and rapacity. Viking marauders attacked England, Ireland, and France, while other groups were busy overrunning the islands of the north – Shetland, Orkney, the Hebrides, and the Faroe Islands; and these attacks increased in weight and organization throughout the ninth century.

No obstacles of land or sea could halt this race of farmer-sailors, it seemed. They rounded Spain and fought in the Mediterranean, in Italy, in North Africa, in Arabia. They hauled their boats overland from the Baltic and made their way down the great Russian rivers and into the Black Sea. They sailed north round the Scandinavian peninsula and reached the White Sea.

But although the so-called Viking Age persisted right into the eleventh century, the nature of the invasions was already changing in the ninth century; many of the raiders were now sailing west with the intention of settling down and establishing communities and kingdoms of their own, spurred on from behind by overpopulation at home and the unwelcome growth of royal power in Scandinavia. Land, not plunder, became their primary aim;

and in the latter half of the ninth century, just when the land-hunger of the Scandinavian emigrants was at its keenest, the Norsemen reached Iceland. In retrospect, this was hardly surprising. The northern seas were now swarming with sturdy ocean-going boats which, although remarkably seaworthy, were often at the mercy of contrary winds. They were not the lean predatory longships built only for coastal waters, but high-stemmed and broad-breasted cargo boats propelled by one large rectangular sail and steered by a long rudder pinned to the star-board quarter. The men who sailed them had neither compass nor lodestone; they could hold course accurately on a latitude, by observing the sun and stars, but they had no way of reck-oning longitude. Their ships, in good weather, were perhaps the fastest craft in the world at that time (it has been estimated that they could make about ten knots); but, more significantly for this story, they were unable to sail very near the wind, and often had difficulty in holding course in a crosswind.

It was this vulnerability to adverse winds, according to the early Icelandic historians, that led to the first Norse sighting of Iceland by storm-driven sailors on their way west from Scandinavia about the year 860. It is, however, just as likely that the Norse discovery of Iceland was no mere accident, as the exis-tence of the country had been known to geographers in Europe long before the Viking Age dawned. The island of *Thule*, which is mentioned by certain Greek and Roman geographers like Strabo and Pytheas of Marseille, may possibly have referred to Iceland, although it should be borne in mind that the designa-tion was also applied to Scandinavia, Shetland, and even the Faroes. But in Anglo-Saxon England the existence of Iceland was well known to the learned writers of the period; in several works, Thule is described as 'the farthest land northwest of Ireland' (Orosius), 'known to few people because of its remote-ness' (Boethius), and 'six days' journey across the sea'; and in the works of the Venerable Bede (672–735), the term Thule unmistakably refers to Iceland, as can be seen from the latitude he assigns it to.

These Anglo-Saxon references probably owe their origin, ulti-mately, to Irish sources. In the sixth century the Celtic Church in Ireland was a centre of remarkable missionary activity. Irish missionaries moved relentlessly up the western coasts of Scotland, founding centres such as Iona and Applecross. The missionary impetus carried them as far as Orkney and Shetland. But in addition to organized missionary expeditions, Irish anchorites were quartering the northern seas in their frail curraghs in search of empty islands where they could cultivate solitude, and shortly after 700 they reached the then-uninhabited Faroes – the last stepping-stone on the way to Iceland.

Then in 825 the Irish monk Dicuil, who was associated with the court of King Charlemagne, wrote a geographical treatise in Latin (*Liber de mensura orbis terrae*) in which he gives an interesting description of Thule based on information given him by three Irish monks who had gone there in 795 – just about the time of the first Viking assaults on Ireland. Dicuil's Thule is quite clearly Iceland; the presence of a few Irish monks in Iceland when the first Norsemen arrived there in 860 is confirmed by the early Icelandic historians, and the existence of place-names like Papey and Papyli corroborates their evidence.

Whether the first Norsemen to set foot on Iceland discovered the country by accident or had learned of its existence previously in Ireland is a debatable point; but their reports of a new country in the north inspired other men of enterprise who came on voyages of planned exploration to size up the prospects of settling there. In 870 a Norwegian named Ingolf Arnarson, impelled to take hasty leave of his homeland because of a killing, became Iceland's first permanent settler, making his home on the site of the present capital, Reykjavik. A host of immigrants of Norse and Celtic stock followed him, and within sixty years the Age of Settlement, as it is called, was over. By 930, it has been estimated, Iceland had a population of perhaps 30,000 and had developed into a nation; in that year there was established a parliamentary commonwealth which lasted for more than 300 years, a unique republican system of aristo-democratic government based on a national assembly (the *Althing*). This was a judicial and legislative body controlled by thirty-six (later thirty-nine) chieftains (*goðar*) whose authority was both secular and religious; but their status was ultimately dependent on the voluntary allegiance of the individual free-holding farmers who were the core of the community.

Once a stable political pattern had evolved in Iceland, it was not very long before this island which had once been an outpost of the Scandinavian sea routes became itself a centre of further exploration: so much so that less than a century later the Icelanders made a treaty with King Olaf Haraldsson of Norway (1014–30), in which they stipulated that Icelanders who were on exploring expeditions and happened to be blown off course to the shores of Norway should not have to pay the customary tax imposed on those entering the country (*landaurar*). And in the next century, Spitzbergen was discovered by sailors on their way from Iceland to Norway, some time before 1170; and Jan Mayen Island, according to the *Icelandic Annals*, was discovered in 1194.

The young, growing nation of Iceland never cultivated isolation. Right from the start, it was very much part of Europe; the sea was a road rather than a barrier. Iceland had limited natural resources, and had to depend largely on foreign trade, with Norway and England as its main customers. From the earliest days, Iceland exported wool, tweed, sheepskins, hides, cheese, tallow, falcons, and sulphur in exchange for timber, tar, metals, flour, malt, honey, wine, beer, and linen.

But Iceland also had a very important 'invisible' export at this time – court poetry. From the tenth century onwards, every single known court poet in Scandinavia came from Iceland, and Icelandic poets could also trade their songs of praise to the earls of Orkney and to princes in England and Norse-speaking Dublin, such was the linguistic affinity of the nations of northern Europe of the time.

Eulogies were sold to fame-hungry kings for hard cash; but the many travelling poets of Iceland also brought back to their country an intimate knowledge of foreign parts. It is indeed one of the striking features of early Icelandic literature how soberly and often accurately northern and western Europe is described. Many of the sagas are partly set in foreign lands, and on the whole they present a plausible picture of even the farthest peoples and places. It is a misconception to think of these Icelandic sources as being primarily 'legendary' or 'fantastic'. Those who are inclined to doubt the authenticity of the voyages described in the Vinland Sagas overlook the fact that we are dealing with a literary genre where the geographical setting of the stories was particularly important, because one of the functions of the sagas was to enlighten their audiences about the past and the present as well as to entertain them.

The Icelandic geographers of the early Middle Ages showed an astonishing sophistication in their image of the northern world. This is how it is described in an Icelandic *Geographical Treatise* preserved in a MS. dating from about 1300, but evidently based on a twelfth-century original:

To the north of Norway lies Finnmark [Lapland]; from there the land sweeps north-east and east to Bjarmaland [Permia], which renders tribute to the king of Russia. From Permia there is uninhabited land stretching all the way to the north until Greenland begins. To the south of Greenland lies Helluland [Baffin Island?] and then Markland [Labrador?]; and from there it is not far to Vinland [America], which some people think extends from Africa.

England and Scotland are one island, but are separate kingdoms; Ireland is a large island. Iceland is also a large island, to the north of Ireland. These islands are all in that part of the world called Europe.

This picture of the north and far west in relation to Europe is drawn with considerable knowledge. In particular, the descriptions of the Arctic regions (stretching from Russia to Greenland) and the eastern seaboard of the North American continent are nowhere to be found in contemporary geographical textbooks elsewhere in Europe – in which they were to remain *terrae incognitae* for a very long time. Nor was there anything esoteric about this geographical knowledge. It was based on the actual experience of Icelandic sailors; another geographical sketch from the twelfth century enshrines the current navigational practices in the northern seas of that time. It is found in the Prologue to *Landnámabók* (Book of Settlements), which describes the settlement of Iceland during the period A.D. 870–930 and was originally compiled in the twelfth century:

According to learned men, it is seven days' sail from Stad in Norway to Horn in the east of Iceland; and from Snæfellsness [on the west coast of Iceland] it is four days' sail to Cape Farewell in Greenland. From Hern Island, off Norway, one can sail due west to Cape Farewell, passing north of Shetland close enough to see it clearly in good visibility, and south of the Faroes half-sunk below the horizon, and a day's sail to the south of Iceland.

From Reykjaness in the south of Iceland it is five days' sail to Slyne Head in Ireland.

From Langaness in the north of Iceland it is four days' sail to Jan Mayen Island, at the end of the ocean, and a day's sail from Kolbeins Island [to the north of Iceland] to the uninhabited regions of Greenland.

It should be clear from all this that the Icelandic writers of the twelfth and thirteenth centuries knew what they were talking about when they described sea journeys and distant lands – and knew better than any other contemporary European writers. The sea routes to the north, south, east, and west had all been explored and charted. Their very clear and detailed picture of the north had begun to emerge a full two centuries earlier, from a mixture of accidental sightings and planned voyages of exploration.

Organized voyages of exploration from Iceland did not start until late in the tenth century. Before that, there had been no need to seek fresh horizons. But after Iceland became fully settled, and certain areas even became over-populated, the urge to find new and more fertile countries stirred again. It is here that the next decisive westward stage is reached, the second-last stepping-stone round the northern rim of the Atlantic towards the New World – the colonization of Greenland. And it is at this point that the story of Vinland really starts in the two sagas presented in this volume.

*

Once again, the first sighting of new land appears to have been accidental. According to *Landnámabók*, round about the year 900 an Icelander named Gunnbjorn Ulfsson was storm-swept into unknown waters far to the west of Iceland; here he came upon some skerries, and caught a glimpse of land even farther to the west. These skerries, which were named Gunnbjarnar Skerries after him, have with reasonable confidence been identified with a group of rocky islets off the east coast of Greenland in the region of Angmagssalik.

Apparently no one made any attempt to follow up Gunnbjorn's discovery for many years. It was not until 978, when the western districts of Iceland were fully settled, that the possibility of living on Greenland itself was investigated. A ship-load of prospective colonists landed on its bitterly inhospitable east coast, and spent an appalling winter snowed up there. Trouble broke out among the members of the expedition, culminating in murder, after which the survivors returned to Iceland to face a savage vengeance. The story of this expedition was told in *Snæbjorn Galti's Saga*, which is no longer extant, but a condensed summary of the saga is incorporated in *Landnámabók*.

Neither of the two Vinland Sagas make any reference to this unhappy expedition led by Snæbjorn Galti. Their account of the discovery and colonization of Greenland begins with the arrival of Eirik the Red, who first went to Greenland in either 981 or 982. Like Iceland's first settler, Ingolf Arnarson, Eirik and his father had emigrated to Iceland from Norway 'because of some killings', as the sagas put it; this was around the year 960. But Iceland was fully settled by then, and it was hard for newcomers to establish themselves. By means of an ambitious marriage, Eirik moved south from the barren land he had settled in the north-west corner of Iceland; but soon his sword involved him in trouble again and he was banished from his new home in the prosperous valley of Haukadale. After some further skirmishing with his neighbours on the islands of Breidafjord, on the west coast, he was declared an outlaw, and with a vengeful band of enemies hard on his heels he decided to sail due west in search of the country Gunnbjorn Ulfsson had sighted nearly a century earlier.

The course he set for Greenland, 200 miles away, was due west on roughly the sixty-fifth parallel, and must have been established by Gunnbjorn Ulfsson himself. Perhaps Eirik had the failure of Snæbjorn Galti's expedition in mind, because when he sighted the towering 6,000-foot glacier of Ingolfsfjeld on the east coast of Greenland he made no attempt to land there, but turned south and rounded Cape Farewell. He spent three years exploring the more inviting west coast, and liked it sufficiently to think of settling there; so back he went to Iceland for a final brush with his enemies and to raise a colonizing expedition, and prudently he named the country *Greenland* ('he said that people would be much more tempted to go there if it had an attractive name'). As a result of his account, he found no lack of volunteers in the western districts of Iceland to answer his call; and in the summer of 985 or 986 a fleet of twenty-five ships carrying several hundred prospective settlers who had sold up their farms in Iceland set sail for Greenland.

Was it all just a confidence trick by a salesman eager to build himself an empire? 'Greenland' is a misnomer for the icy regions of that huge new country, and it is easy to suspect that Eirik the Red deliberately misled his countrymen – particularly when we read (*Grænlendinga Saga*, Chapter 1) that only fourteen of the fleet of twenty-five ships reached their destination, although some of the others got safely back to Iceland. But it is clear from the saga that the fleet encountered freakish weather – perhaps a submarine earthquake – to account for this initial disaster. It is also clear from all the evidence available that the climate of the north from the ninth to the twelfth centuries was warmer than it is even now, and did not begin to deteriorate until the fourteenth century. Eirik's crossing to Greenland was no holiday cruise; but it was not until the fourteenth century that sailors were forced to abandon the old route from Snæfellsness to Angmagssalik entirely, because of the increasing danger of polar ice.

Most of the settlers established themselves in the Julianehaab area (the 'Eastern Settlement' of the sagas); there were 190 farms in this area, loosely grouped around Eirik the Red's large farm at Brattahlid, in Eiriksfjord (modern Tunugdliarfik), and these first settlers acknowledged Eirik's patriarchal authority. The rest of the colonists pushed 200 miles farther north-west up the coast, and created the 'Western Settlement' of ninety farms in the Godthaab area.

The conditions in Greenland at this time were probably not very unlike those in Iceland – a little more severe, perhaps. There was sufficient grassland to allow animal husbandry on the coastal strip between the sea and the monstrous glaciers of the interior, and the fjords and rivers abounded with fish. The Greenlanders also caught larger game like reindeer, seals, walrus, whales, and polar bears. They raised sheep, cattle, ponies, pigs, and goats but they were always dependent on foreign trade for many of the major necessities of life – corn, for instance, and timber and iron; and in return they exported walrus ivory, skins, hides, furs, and ship's ropes made from walrus hides.

The Norse sites in Greenland have been very carefully excavated by Danish archaeologists, who have painstakingly uncovered a most vivid picture of medieval Norse life. Hundreds of dwellings have been excavated, and the size of the farms shows that these two communities on the west coast of Greenland between the sixtieth and sixty-fifth parallel were reasonably prosperous: for instance, Eirik's farm at Brattahlid had four barns and room for forty head of cattle.

It has been estimated that the total population of Greenland, at the height of its Norse colonization, was something like 3,000. Greenland was an independent nation, with a constitution of its own closely modelled on that of Iceland: it had an annual National Assembly at Gardar (modern Igaliko) which, like its Icelandic counterpart, was both legislative and judicial in its function and was presided over by a Law-Speaker.

Christianity was introduced from Iceland shortly after the year 1000 (the year in which Iceland itself adopted Christianity by parliamentary decree), although there seems to be no basis of historical fact for the statement in *Eirik's Saga*, Chapter 5, that Eirik's son, Leif the Lucky, was the evangelizing agent working at the behest of King Olaf Tryggvason of Norway (see below, p. 32). For the first century the Church seems to have been rather haphazardly organized; Greenland was probably visited by missionary bishops from Iceland until the Greenland bishopric was established in 1126. At Gardar, in the Eastern Settlement, the remains of a stone cathedral nearly a hundred feet long can still be seen. Sixteen other parish churches of stone have been uncovered, and in the 1960s archaeologists came across the remains of a very early church of wood and turf, identified as the tiny little chapel built near Brattahlid by Eirik's wife, Thjodhild (*Eirik's Saga*, Chapter 5). This is the earliest datable Norse church that has been found anywhere in the Scandinavian world, and is only one more example of the immensely valuable archaeological material that Greenland has yielded.

People are apt to think of Greenland as lying beyond the farthest beyond, and find it exceptionally hard to imagine it as having sustained a flourishing European community long before Chaucer's day. Greenland was to a large degree an extension of Icelandic civilization, and the two countries were closely linked by bonds of culture and kinship. Many of the early bishops of the Greenland Church came from Iceland, and there was considerable communication between the two countries.

To Icelanders of the period, life in Greenland held a certain fascination; to them it was rather an exotic country, although not an unfamiliar one. Apart from the two Vinland Sagas, Greenland forms the background for episodes in several other Icelandic sagas. For example, *Fóstbrœðra Saga* (The Blood-Brothers' Saga) describes how an Icelandic poet went to Greenland in pursuit of the man who had killed his blood-brother – and for the purposes of the narrative, no doubt, it is the hardship of life in Greenland that is stressed. *Kroka-Ref's Saga* tells the story of a man who had to flee from Iceland because of a killing and lived for a while in Greenland; it describes, among other things, how Kroka-Ref built himself a stronghold there and led water into it through a wooden conduit – and similar devices from the Norse period in Greenland have now been revealed there by archaeologists. *Flóamanna Saga* tells the very moving story of a man named Thorgils who set sail for Greenland with the intention of settling there. His ship ran into difficulties, the crew were faced with starvation in the frozen sea, his wife gave birth to a son and was later brutally murdered; but Thorgils struggled on bravely and managed to keep his newborn son alive until they finally made land in Greenland. But life there did not turn out as he had expected and, bitterly disillusioned, he returned to Iceland where he settled down on his old farm and went back to cultivating his former home-field.

The *Tale of Einar Sokkason* describes in detail how the Greenland bishopric was founded in 1126, and gives an interesting general picture of life there in the twelfth century. *Poet-Helgi's Saga*, which is now lost in its original form but survives in a later metrical version, also deals with events in Greenland.

These and other sagas suggest the keen interest taken by the Icelandic saga-writers in the affairs of this little-sister country and afford us a considerable insight into conditions there. One intriguing reference comes from inside Greenland itself. It is from a letter written in the year 1266 by a Greenlandic priest named Halldor to a colleague and compatriot who was at that time living in Norway; the original is lost, but its contents are known from a later MS. The letter describes how some Greenlanders had that year travelled farther north into the hinterland than anyone had ever gone before. It recounts observations made by the explorers which show that they had paused at a place whose latitude was $75°\ 46'$ north; the expedition had then gone another three days' journey farther north. That the Greenlanders were careful explorers of the northern regions far within the Arctic circle is corroborated by an incomplete runic inscription that has been found on a cairn at latitude $72°\ 55'$, in the Kingiktorssoak region, dating from the early fourteenth century:

Erling Sighvatsson and Bjarni Thordarson and Eindridi Jonsson, on the Saturday before the minor Rogation Day [April 25], built these cairns, and cleared . . .

But by this time, the Norse colonization of Greenland had entered its decline. In 1261, Greenland lost its independence; it succumbed to the political power of Norway, just as Iceland was to do the following year, and its trade, now monopolized by the Norwegian crown, immediately took a turn for the worse. The king of Norway contracted to send two ships a year to Greenland, and forbade any other trade to take place; but there is no record of any royal ship leaving Norway for Greenland after the year 1367. The decline in Greenland's fortunes can be largely attributed to this political setback: Greenland simply was not prosperous enough to be able to afford to pay tribute to an alien country.

But there was worse to come; in addition to the loss of independence, the Greenlanders were soon to be faced with two enemies they had no means of overcoming – a rapid and terrifying deterioration in the climate, and the return of the Inuit whose culture was so much better suited to withstand the colder conditions.

According to the earliest extant work on Icelandic history – Ari Thorgilsson's *Íslendingabók* (Book of Icelanders), written around 1127 – the first Norse settlers in Greenland had come across traces of indigenous inhabitants whom they called *Skrælings*, and it is clear that these were the seal-hunting Inuit aborigines who had migrated farther north as the climate had improved throughout the northern hemisphere after the Ice Age. But with the return of more severe conditions the Inuit began to move south again. While the Scandinavian dynamic was declining all over Europe in the fourteenth century, the Inuit attacked and wiped out the Western Settlement in Greenland, and began to harry the surviving Norsemen farther south.

The *Icelandic Annals*, which contain frequent if brief references to Greenland during the period 1121–1410, record this grimly laconic entry for the year 1379:

Skrælings attacked the Greenlanders, killing eighteen of them and carrying off two boys into captivity.

As the sea ice tightened its grip round the coasts of Greenland, the remaining Eastern Settlement was completely cut off from the rest of the civilized world. The last reference to Greenland in the contemporary *Icelandic Annals* is for 1410, when an Icelander returned home after spending four years in Greenland. He may, in fact, have caught the last ship from Greenland, for there is no record of further sailings from there after that. In a Papal letter written in 1492 there is corroborative evidence for this conjecture, because it says:

It is said that Greenland is an island near the edge of the world and that its inhabitants have neither bread, wine, nor oils, and live on dried fish and milk. Because of the ice that surrounds the island, sailings there are rare, because land can only be made there in August when the ice has receded. For that reason it is thought that no ship has sailed there for the last eighty years, and no bishop nor priest has been there [for that period]. As a consequence, most of the inhabitants have abandoned their Christian faith, and the only remembrance they still preserve of it is that once a year they exhibit the corporal that was used by their last bishop about a hundred years ago.

Archaeological evidence of grave-finds reveals a grim story of progressive deterioration in this hardy Norse colony.

By the end of the fifteenth century, when this new Ice Age was at its most intense, the last beleaguered Norsemen had degenerated into a stunted, puny race, ravaged by disease and deformed by malnutrition, but still clinging to the remnants of their Christian culture. It is unlikely that any of them survived into the sixteenth century. It is a tragic irony of history that this exhausted outpost of Norse exploration, just beyond the fringe of European endurance, should have died such a horrible and lonely death while a new age of exploration was dawning in southern Europe; because at the time when the colony founded by Eirik the Red, father of the first explorer of America, was coming to its end, Christopher Columbus was rediscovering the New World.

*

It was the colonization of Greenland that brought the Norsemen within striking distance of America. And once again, the pattern established by the discovery of Iceland and Greenland was repeated: chance sighting (by Bjarni Herjolfsson), followed by planned exploration (by Leif the Lucky), and then planned settlement (by Thorfinn Karlsefni).[1]

1. It has sometimes been suggested that the Irish were the first white people to discover America, but this claim is based on the flimsiest of evidence – the semi-legendary descriptions of faraway islands recorded in the Irish voyages and other related literature like the Life of St Brendan. Despite the inconclusiveness of the evidence, however, the possibility that the Irish reached America cannot be ruled out entirely, in view of the tenacity and daring seamanship with which Irish anchorites sailed in search of solitude.

The two Vinland Sagas are the only sources which give a detailed account of these explorations; and it is perhaps this fact, coupled with a certain confusion about the nature of the Icelandic sagas as a literary genre, which has led to the assumption that there is no real basis for believing that Vinland was part of America, or indeed that it ever existed at all. Yet no one would attempt to deny that Iceland itself was settled by the Norsemen, or that Greenland supported a large Norse colony for 500 years; and the evidence for the discovery and colonization of Vinland comes from the same kind of sources – the Icelandic sagas. We have already seen how sophisticated the saga-writers were in their knowledge of the outside world, and how much of the impetus for northern exploration came from Iceland itself; in the light of all this, it is surely perverse to doubt the authenticity of Vinland.

But, as it happens, the Vinland Sagas are not the only historical sources that record the fact that Vinland was discovered, nor are they by any means the earliest. *Grœnlendinga Saga* was apparently written in the late twelfth century, more than 150 years after the events it relates, and *Eirik's Saga* was probably not written until the middle of the thirteenth century; but the earliest extant reference to Vinland was written down only about sixty years after Thorfinn Karlsefni had gone there.

It was made by a German priest named Adam of Bremen who, around the year 1075, completed a monumental history in Latin of the Archbishopric of Hamburg (*Gesta Hammaburgensis ecclesiae pontificum*).

Less than ten years previously, Adam had visited the royal court of Denmark to gain information about the peoples of Scandinavia, because, until 1104, they came under the ecclesiastical jurisdiction of the Archbishopric of Bremen and Hamburg; his main informant in Denmark was King Svein Ulfsson, nephew of King Canute the Great. In the section that deals with the history and geography of Scandinavia, those 'islands of the north' as he called them (*Descriptio insularum Aquilonis*, Chapter 38), Adam wrote that King Svein

24

recounted that there was another island in that ocean which had been discovered by many and was called *Vinland*, because vines grow wild there and yield excellent wine, and, moreover, self-sown grain grows there in abundance; it is not from any fanciful imaginings that we have learned this, but from the reliable reports of the Danes.

The royal courts of Scandinavia were the focal points of cultural and learned activity, and it is not surprising that news of Vinland should have reached them. *Grænlendinga Saga* itself (Chapter 3) recounts that Bjarni Herjolfsson, the man who first sighted America, later went to Norway and told Earl Eirik about his voyage across the Atlantic and the various lands he had sighted; and coming even closer to Adam of Bremen's time, we know that his informant, King Svein Ulfsson, had recently received a visitor from Greenland – an Icelander named Audun, who had travelled all the way from Greenland to Denmark to present the king with a polar bear (the tale of his journey, *Audun's Tale*, is one of the most delightful short stories in world literature).

Whatever King Svein's actual source was, the information he gave Adam of Bremen contains significant corroboration of the Vinland Sagas, both of which refer to the wild grapes and wild wheat whose abundance so pleased the first Norse explorers – and which also caught the attention of the next wave of explorers from Europe in the sixteenth century. Both grain and wine had to be imported to Iceland and Greenland, so that it is not surprising that the merchant-adventurers who went to Vinland should emphasize these particular features in their accounts. And Adam's phrase 'discovered by many' bears out the impression from the sagas that there were a number of separate expeditions to Vinland.

About the same time as Adam of Bremen was seeking information about the north from King Svein of Denmark, there was born in Iceland, in 1067, a man named Ari Thorgilsson, Iceland's first historian in the vernacular. Ari is one of the most important figures in Iceland's medieval literature, and much of our knowledge of the early history of the country is derived directly or indirectly from him. He was brought up among people whose memories stretched far back into the years of the so-called Saga

Age (930–1030), and tutored by scholarly clerics who combined a European breadth of education with a close interest in Iceland's history. To the lore of the pagan past in which he had been steeped from boyhood, Ari applied a mind carefully trained in the new learning of the Christian cultural world. In his historical writing he showed a scrupulous concern for accuracy, weighing his sources judiciously and integrating events in Iceland into the framework of European history; it was not for nothing that he was known as Ari the Learned.

Ari was probably one of the compilers of the original version of *Landnámabók*, which now survives only in several later versions. At the request of the two bishops of Iceland he produced, somewhere around the year 1127, his vernacular history of the Icelandic people – *Íslendingabók* (or *Libellus Islandorum*, the Book of Icelanders) – which appears to be a summarized version of a fuller account which is no longer extant. It is worth noting that one of the bishops concerned in this commissioning of Ari's history was Bishop Thorlak Runolfsson, whose mother was the granddaughter of Thorfinn Karlsefni (cf. the genealogies in the closing chapters of both the Vinland Sagas); and it can hardly be doubted that traditions about Karlsefni's expedition to Vinland had been kept alive in the bishop's family.

In *Íslendingabók*, Ari devotes a brief section to Greenland, quoting as his authority his uncle Thorkel Gellison, who had once been to Greenland and had talked there to one of the original settlers who had gone out with Eirik the Red:

Eirik the Red went out to colonize Greenland fourteen or fifteen years before Christianity came to Iceland [i.e. 985 or 986], according to what Thorkel Gellison was told in Greenland by a man who had himself gone there with Eirik the Red.

Ari also makes a passing reference to Vinland in this section, in connexion with some traces of human habitation which the first settlers in Greenland discovered – a reference which, though brief, is strikingly significant, not least because Ari takes it for granted that the mention of Vinland itself should need no further elaboration for Icelandic readers:

The country named Greenland was discovered and colonized from Iceland. A man called Eirik the Red, from Breidafjord, went there and took possession of land in the district which has since been called Eiriksfjord. He gave the country a name and called it *Greenland*, and said that people would be the more eager to go there if it had an attractive name.

They found there human habitations, both in the Eastern and Western parts of the country, and fragments of skin-boats and stone implements; from which it can be concluded that the people who had been there before were of the same kind as those who inhabit *Vinland* and whom the Greenlanders call *Skrælings*.

This twelfth-century identification of the Inuit natives of Greenland with the Native Americans of North America, based on the similarity between two primitive material cultures, is an interesting deduction. The term *Skræling* means something like 'wretch', a contemptuous term applied to the indigenous natives of a country, rather like 'savages'. It is quite clear from the Vinland Sagas that the Skrælings of North America were not the same as the Inuit of Greenland, however, but Native Americans; apart from the physical characteristics of broad cheek-bones and black hair, most of the incidental details given about various aspects of Skræling life are recognizable; ethnologists who have studied the early Native American tribes of the eastern seaboard of North America have found corroboration in the habits of many tribes.

The Algonquins, for instance, used a 'ballista', which consisted of a heavy boulder sewed in a skin and fastened to a pole, and could create a lot of damage; this tallies closely with the catapults described in *Eirik's Saga*, Chapter 11. Although birch canoes were commonplace among Native Americans, canoes made of moose-hide were known, as was the practice of sleeping under them (*Grænlendinga Saga*, Chapter 5). *Eirik's Saga* (Chapter 11) also describes Native American food as being 'deer-marrow mixed with blood' – a fair description of the pemmican used by hunting tribes.

But the most familiar aspect of the Skræling episodes is surely the way in which these first European colonists treated the natives they met. In their early trading encounters, they exploited the natives mercilessly, gaining all manner of pelts and furs in exchange for measures of milk or tiny strips of red cloth.

But the Skrælings had the last word, evidently. Despite the Norsemen's superiority of weapons, it was the constant threat of attack by the natives that finally discouraged the attempt to colonize Vinland.

A century after Thorfinn Karlsefni went to Vinland, its exact location seems to have been forgotten: the *Icelandic Annals* have an entry for the year 1121 – 'Bishop Eirik of Greenland went in search of Vinland' – which implies that the old sailing directions had become confused. But all contacts with the North American continent did not cease; the *Annals* relate that in the year 1347 a ship that had been to Markland (Labrador?) was driven off course on its way back to Greenland and eventually found haven in Iceland, anchorless and with seventeen survivors on board. Timber from Markland, apparently, was not unknown in Greenland for centuries after the Vinland expeditions; archaeologists have discovered, at Herjolfsness (modern Ikagait), chests made of larch, which was unknown in Scandinavia but abundant in Labrador and Newfoundland.

Even after the written records peter out, there is good reason to believe that a continuing knowledge about North America survived in Iceland at least, if not in Greenland. Maps made in Iceland a century after Columbus rediscovered America still used the pre-Columban Norse names (cf. Stefansson's map, on p. 121), and showed the promontory of Vinland on the main coastline at roughly the same latitude as Newfoundland. And in 1625 an Icelander named Bjorn Jonsson who had borrowed *Hauksbók* (one of the two main manuscripts of *Eirik's Saga*) added a little note about Markland:

From the innermost shores of Markland comes driftwood. Markland is so called because of its dense forests. . . .

Although it would be unwise to be dogmatic, the likeliest identification of Markland is the coast of Labrador. And for someone living on the west coast of Greenland, Labrador was just as accessible as Norway, and the sea voyage via Baffin Island no more dangerous than the North Sea crossing along the sixtieth parallel from Cape Farewell to Bergen. Once it is accepted that the Norsemen knew for certain that there was land to the west (and their geographical writings prove this beyond all doubt), the rest of the story follows quite logically, and it is safe to assume that voyages to Labrador to fetch timber continued for a long time; it had not been the distance that had deterred colonization, but the Native Americans. Unlike Columbus, the Norsemen were not sailing on an act of faith.

Even if the two Vinland Sagas did not exist today, there would still be ample indications to suggest that the Norsemen had been to the North American continent, as a matter of bare history. The real significance of the sagas is that they so greatly enlarge our knowledge and understanding of the event itself: they illuminate history with humanity.

They do not pretend to be strictly historical or geographical treatises, and the historian who treats them primarily as such must inevitably be disappointed, since many of the details he or she would like to find are missing or muddled. This is because the saga-writers were concerned, basically, with people; the events are described through the experiences of the men and women involved in the adventure. It is the historical interest of the Vinland Sagas that has made them so famous, but their historical value cannot be properly assessed without reference to their literary context.

*

The oldest surviving text of *Grænlendinga Saga* was copied out some two centuries after the saga was originally written. It is found in *Flateyjarbók*, the largest of the Icelandic vellum codices, which contains a wide collection of saga material of all kinds. It was written down in the north of Iceland between 1382 and 1395 for a wealthy Icelandic farmer named Jon Hakonarson, and was cherished as a family heirloom for generation after generation until a descendant gave it to an Icelandic bishop who in turn presented it to the King of Denmark in the seventeenth century; it was returned to Iceland in 1971 and is now in the Arnamagnæan Institute in Reykjavik. There are also four paper copies, derived from *Flateyjarbók*.

Eirik's Saga survives in two vellum manuscripts. The older of the two is *Hauksbók*, a large codex of sagas and learned writings which was compiled in Iceland early in the fourteenth century by Hauk Erlendsson the Lawman, who shared the work of transcription with two secretaries. The other vellum text is found in *Skálholtsbók*, a codex dating from the late fifteenth century. Both these vellums are now in the Arnamagnæan Institute in Reykjavik. There are also five seventeenth-century paper transcripts of the *Hauksbók* text.

Both the main texts of *Eirik's Saga* derive from a common source, but there are considerable stylistic differences between them. For many years, scholars were inclined to believe that *Hauksbók* preserved the more faithful image of the original; the style is much more polished and the writing is of a high standard, whereas the scribe of *Skálholtsbók* was often careless in his copying and his text is marred by a number of slipshod errors. Medieval scribes varied greatly; some were content to copy slavishly, even when they did not fully understand the text before them, while others indulged in extensive editing.

The Swedish scholar Sven B. F. Jansson, in his book *Sagorna om Vinland* (vol. 1, Lund, 1944), made a detailed comparison of the two manuscripts which proved conclusively that *Hauksbók*, far from being the more faithful copy of the original, had been extensively edited and revised by Hauk Erlendsson and his two secretaries. He discovered that when Hauk Erlendsson himself wielded the pen, the saga had been drastically shortened (by twenty-five per cent), and that where the handwriting of the second secretary took over, the saga had been considerably lengthened (by fifteen per cent); whereas in the passages for which the first secretary had been responsible very little tampering had taken place – only a lengthening by some three per cent.

The general effect of this revision was to give the saga in *Hauksbók* a more 'classical' tone: archaic words and colloquial idioms alike were discarded, stylistic repetitions were avoided, perfunctory sentences were expanded and rounded, and much of the dialogue was given a more terse, epigrammatic tone. Hauk Erlendsson was a cultivated gentleman of impeccable literary tastes; he lived in the aftermath of the golden age of saga-writing in the thirteenth century, and he made a deliberate attempt to 'improve' the saga according to his conception of what a good saga should be like. Also, he had a special interest in *Eirik's Saga*, since he himself was descended from Thorfinn Karlsefni, the Icelander who led the colonizing expedition to Vinland. For that reason, he inserted additional genealogical material into the text (Chapters 7 and 14), and made several slight alterations designed to add further lustre to his ancestor's fame.

The scribe of *Skálholtsbók* had no such literary pretensions; his text is longer and somewhat garbled in places, but it is unquestionably more faithful to his original than the *Hauksbók* text is, and for that reason this present translation of *Eirik's Saga* has been based on *Skálholtsbók* and not, as previous translations have been, on *Hauksbók*.

Nevertheless, it is still impossible to know for certain how close we are to the saga as it was originally written. Both texts had a common source, but that may have been several removes from the original manuscript; it is quite clear that somewhere along the line the original opening to the saga was discarded, because the first two chapters have been lifted directly from another source – *Landnámabók*. It must always be borne in mind that the Icelandic sagas were never museum pieces, embalming for all time a literary act; they were living things, and later generations thought nothing of adapting or re-writing them to suit changing tastes.

Grœnlendinga Saga, too, suffered changes. It is no longer to be found anywhere in one piece. The existing version in *Flateyjarbók* had been rather clumsily incorporated into the so-called *Great Saga of Olaf Tryggvason*; this is a vast, sprawling compilation of historical material which had accrued round the biography of King Olaf Tryggvason of Norway, put together some time in the early fourteenth century. King Olaf was the man who in his short reign (995–1000) converted Norway to the Christian faith by force as much as persuasion, and his importance as the founder of the Scandinavian Church explains the great interest taken in him by the ecclesiastically trained writers of the Middle Ages. *Grœnlendinga Saga* was roughly tailored into this patchwork compilation, and in the process its opening chapters were lost and are no longer extant; as in *Eirik's Saga*, the first chapter of *Grænlendinga Saga* as it has come down to us is an interpolation borrowed from a late version of *Landnámabók*.

Thus, neither *Grænlendinga Saga* nor *Eirik's Saga*, as we know them now, is in its original form, and this has done nothing to ease the task of the historian.

In addition to the questions raised by the provenance of the texts, there is the very large problem of the differences between the two sagas. In the past, *Eirik's Saga* has been preferred by most scholars where its account differed from that of *Grænlendinga Saga*, chiefly on the ground that *Eirik's Saga* (particularly the *Hauksbók* text) approximated more closely to the 'classical' saga – and therefore, presumably, was a more reliable source. But the relationship between the two sagas has now been clarified beyond all doubt by the researches of the late Professor Jón Jóhannesson of Iceland ('Aldur Grænlendinga Sögu', in *Nordæla*, Reykjavik, 1956).

Roughly speaking, the two sagas describe the same historical events and the same historical personages; but the key difference lies in the role played by Leif the Lucky, son of Eirik the Red. In *Eirik's Saga*, it was Leif who made the first accidental discovery of America, in the year 1000; whereas in *Grænlendinga Saga*, Leif made a planned voyage of exploration to America after it had been accidentally sighted by Bjarni Herjolfsson some fifteen years earlier.

The account in *Eirik's Saga* is very circumstantial (Chapter 5). It says that Leif Eiriksson had spent the winter in Norway, where he had been persuaded by King Olaf Tryggvason to go back to Greenland as his evangelist agent in order to convert Greenland to Christianity; and that in the summer of 1000 he had set sail for Greenland but been blown off course right across the North Atlantic. He discovered unsuspected lands there, where he found wild wheat, vines, and maple trees. On his way back to Greenland he came across some shipwrecked seamen, whom he rescued, and when he reached home he successfully converted the country to Christianity despite opposition from his father; and for all this he became known as Leif the Lucky.

Professor Jóhannesson proved decisively that Leif Eiriksson's Christianizing mission to Greenland on behalf of King Olaf Tryggvason never took place at all, and that the story had been invented late in the twelfth century by an Icelandic monk, Gunnlaug Leifsson, who was engaged in writing a biography of King Olaf. The argument is a complex one, but basically it turns on the number of countries that King Olaf is said to have Christianized during his five-year reign.

The earliest historians all say that King Olaf Tryggvason instigated the conversion of five countries: Norway, Iceland, Orkney, Shetland, and the Faroes. In the late twelfth century, however, a sixth country was added to the tally of those which the king was said to have converted: Greenland. It is significant that the thirteenth-century historians accepted this addition without question, but in some texts a tell-tale discrepancy crept in – the original figure of five would be retained, but six countries would then be listed by name, ending with Greenland.

Many of the original texts are lost, but Professor Jóhannesson demonstrated by deduction that the story of Leif Eiriksson's connexion with this evangelistic work can be traced to one particular monk, Gunnlaug Leifsson, who wrote a (lost) *Olaf Tryggvason's Saga* in Latin about the year 1200; only a few fragments of it now survive, embedded in later works.

The author of *Grænlendinga Saga* clearly knew nothing of this story, and from this it follows that it must have been written earlier than Gunnlaug Leifsson's *Olaf Tryggvason's Saga:* that is to say, it must have been written before the year 1200. The compiler of the *Great Saga of Olaf Tryggvason* in *Flateyjarbók* was aware of the discrepancy between *Grænlendinga Saga* and the Olaf Tryggvason biographies; in an attempt to rationalize or at least minimize the differences, he inserted into the saga a brief section noting that Leif Eiriksson had been christened in Norway and had evangelized Greenland.

The author of *Eirik's Saga*, which was written somewhere around or after the middle of the thirteenth century, was faced with the same problem of reconciling two totally incompatible stories about the first sighting and exploration of America – the account in *Grænlendinga Saga*, and the fable started by the monk Gunnlaug Leifsson. His solution was to recast the saga entirely in the light of what he considered to be more reliable information. He discarded the story of Bjarni Herjolfsson's accidental sighting; but then he also had to discard the story of Leif's deliberate voyage of exploration, with all its circumstantial detail. Some of these details were transferred to other expeditions, all of which had to be rearranged to some extent, and we can find identical episodes in both sagas applied to different situations; for instance, the story of Eirik the Red's fall from his horse is told, in *Grænlendinga Saga* (Chapter 3), in connexion with Leif Eiriksson's voyage, but in *Eirik's Saga* the same episode is told in connexion with Thorstein Eiriksson's voyage (Chapter 5).

It is now quite clear that *Eirik's Saga* was written as a deliberate revision of *Grænlendinga Saga*, and this accounts for some of the major differences between the two sagas. The author of *Eirik's Saga* seems to have been a conscientious historian who believed that he was working with better information about the major characters involved – not only Leif the Lucky, but also Thorfinn Karlsefni and his wife Gudrid. It is possible that he had access to some written records about Gudrid which have not survived; she had many important descendants, and it would be in their interest to ensure that the family history was accurately documented.

Although the sagas contradict one another on several important points, they also complement one another – particularly in the kind of illumination they shed on the personalities of the people involved. They are seen and described from different angles, and this illustrates another fundamental source of difference between the two versions: the difference in the literary standards of the two eras in which they were written. They reflect tastes and techniques which changed considerably in the decades that separated them; and it is this change that was ultimately responsible for their characteristic differences as literary works. Too often, this literary factor has been overlooked because of the outstanding historical interest of the sagas.

*

Saga-writing began early in the twelfth century as an adjunct to the writing of 'learned works' (*frœði*) which was being fostered by the Icelandic Church. Sagas were encouraged as serious popular entertainment in an effort by the church authorities to discourage the grosser forms of popular amusement (such as dancing), and to combat the ignorance of the people. And because of the peculiar social conditions of medieval Iceland, saga-writing quickly developed into a huge national literature.

How did it come about? Take, first, the political situation. As a republic, Iceland had no royal court to attract to it all the available wealth and cultural talent in the country and to form an exclusive, sophisticated audience of its own. Nor was there any royal line on which all literary interest and historical tradition could focus; and so, when Ari the Learned wrote the first vernacular history of Iceland, he had to make a decisive break with the European habit in which he had been trained; he had to write the history of a republic in which all the original settlers had been nominally equal. It was not the ancestors and the exploits of one exclusive ruling family of which he was writing, but the ancestors and exploits of every family in the country. It was this that stimulated the transference into literary form of the great treasury of oral traditions in Iceland; Iceland at that time was young enough to be able to remember its origins with remarkable clarity, without recourse to myth-making. An individual's status still depended to a large extent on the achievements of his immediate ancestors, and his strength within the community was measured by the range and importance of his family connexions as well as by his personal prowess. *Landnámabók*, first compiled early in the twelfth century, is a systematic account of the first settlers of Iceland, district by district; and it helped to liberate a flood of traditions that had been treasured in families all over the country.

Secondly, Iceland had not yet had time to develop a rigid social and cultural caste system. Priests were farmers, aristocrats were priests, farmers were poets, and poets were peasants. Books were never the exclusive possession of any one class, nor was literacy. For instance, the school that was founded at Holar, in the north of Iceland, at the beginning of the twelfth century had a wide scatter of pupils, including women; and mention is specifically made of a church carpenter there, one Thorodd Gamlason, who became highly proficient in Latin. This policy of widespread general education meant that there was a large reservoir of literary capacity available for the conversion of oral material into written sagas.

It was the unique nature of the audience, too, that helped to condition the development of this literature. For many centuries there was not a single village in the whole of Iceland. People lived on farms of varying sizes, often in considerable isolation; the climate and the ruggedness of the terrain forced them to be largely self-supporting units, because in winter, travel of any kind was hazardous and the distance between farms made it prohibitive for all but the most special formal occasions. Thus, the farms not only had to be economically self-supporting, they had to be culturally self-supporting, too. They had to create their own entertainment, for themselves and for their occasional visitors. The favourite pastime was dancing to the music of sung ballads, and the telling of stories about the past and news about the present.

Here the Church took a hand, because it disapproved of dancing and tried to cultivate an alternative entertainment, by distributing books of an edifying nature – lives of saints, homilies, and others. First these were read aloud from the pulpit, and then read aloud by priests making parish visitations; and because of the scattered nature of the parishes, the priests encouraged individual households to undertake the task on their behalf. This created a growing demand for more and more manuscripts so that people could read aloud for themselves. The first bishop of Holar, in the north of Iceland (1106–21), laid great stress on this aspect of educating the people; he established a brisk manuscript-making industry, with a number of copyists fully engaged on the work of transcribing. One of the last questions he was asked when he was lying on his deathbed was what the price of a newly completed book was to be.

It was in this way that writing for the purpose of serious popular entertainment came into being. It struck an immediate response in a people addicted to rummaging through their

genealogies and reminiscing on the tales of the past. It seems to
have been a very short step from the writing of strictly religious
saga-entertainment to secular saga-entertainment; it did not take
long before sagas were being written for specific entertainments,
apparently, like the wedding at Reykholar in 1119, for instance.
On this celebrated occasion, which is described in the *Saga of
Thorgils and Haflidi*, a priest called Ingimund Einarsson and a
farmer called Hrolf of Skalmarness recited sagas which they
themselves had 'composed' – apparently for the purpose of
entertaining the assembled wedding guests. One of these sagas
still survives in a much later metrical version; it was about a
legendary warrior-king called Hromund Gripsson. But the other,
about Orm the Barra-Poet, is now, unfortunately, lost.

That is how saga-writing started: a unique blend of entertainment and learning, fact and fantasy, history and story-telling,
literary endeavour and family pride, pagan past and Christian
present. And it is in this context that we must read *Grænlendinga
Saga*, which was written when this age of saga-literature was still
in its adolescence.

It is a distinctly primitive saga compared with the great classics of the next century such as *Egil's Saga* or *Laxdæla Saga* or
Njal's Saga. The technique is fairly unsophisticated, the narrative
bald; fused in it are many of the rudimentary ingredients which
were part of the initial saga-writing impulse. First and foremost,
it was entertaining, in that it was a good yarn about people of
heroic stature and spectacular achievement. It was educational,
in that it was a form of popular history and geography. It was
also edifying, in that it told the story of the ancestor (Thorfinn
Karlsefni) of three of the bishops of the twelfth century – their
names are carefully recorded in the genealogies of the last
chapter. And at the same time it retained much of the vigorous
coarse-grained pagan nature of popular folk-tale – the ghostly
voice that warns the sleeping explorers of imminent attack
(Chapter 5), the macabre antics of dead bodies that will not rest
in peace (Chapter 6), the apparition of the dark-haired woman
in Vinland (Chapter 7), the blood-thirsty atrocities committed
by Freydis (Chapter 8). Popular taste was informing the rather
austere pattern of literary effort fostered by the early Church

to supplant more ignorant and morally dangerous forms of amusement. Above all, *Grænlendinga Saga* is written uncritically, unselfconsciously – and has all the failings and merits implied in this.

Eirik's Saga is the product of a later and very different literary era. Saga-writing had by then become a highly sophisticated art, coming to a climax in the fifty-year Golden Age between *Egil's Saga* and *Njal's Saga* (1230–80). The author's attitude to his material is now much more critical; where *Grænlendinga Saga* made only a perfunctory claim to authenticity ('It was Karlsefni himself who told more fully than anyone else the story of all these voyages, which has been to some extent recorded here'), there is now a more self-conscious seeking after fact, a carefully-projected attitude of objectivity ('According to some people . . .' in Chapter 11, where the author gives an alternative version). The author clearly made use of various other written sources, such as *Olaf Tryggvason's Saga* and a late version of *Landnámabók*, and he incorporated some of this fresh material into his narrative; even the very fact that he set out to revise *Grænlendinga Saga* is an indication of the changed attitudes of the later thirteenth century.

All the writing techniques have improved. As was the custom in the great classical sagas, the narrative is given a wider historical perspective; the author traces Gudrid's genealogy forward from the roots of Iceland's history – it was Aud the Deep-Minded, that remarkable matriarchal figure, who brought Gudrid's ancestor, Vifil, to Iceland and gave him land to settle on. In construction, the saga is much more tidy and logical than its predecessor, and the sprawling material of the many voyages to Vinland has been compressed into a more manageable form.

The style is very different, too. The writing has greater polish (even in the *Skálholtsbók* text), and the events are more carefully motivated by cause and effect. The whole saga has an air of conscious scholarship. The rather haphazard geography of *Grænlendinga Saga* has been rationalized, and Vinland is now fitted into a proper cartographic context and related also to the abstract theories of the geographers who thought that Vinland might extend to Africa; this is the origin of the episode with the Uniped (Chapter 12), for Unipeds were thought to live in Africa. The episode of the prophetess in Greenland (Chapter 4) is depicted with all the care of an antiquarian, and has provided us with the most detailed description of a sybil vaticinating that survives in Icelandic literature. The Skrælings are described more fully, and there is even an attempt to reproduce occasional Native American names (Chapter 12). Older folk-tale motifs are given an overlay of sophistication: the corpse of Thorstein Eiriksson, which in *Grænlendinga Saga* sat up to prophesy Gudrid's future (Chapter 6), in *Eirik's Saga* delivers a homily about Christian burial (Chapter 6). The overall effect is of much greater experience in saga-writing, the prose more flexible, the narrative brisker, the story-telling more subtle.

As usual, the names of the two saga-authors are unknown to us. We cannot even know for certain where the sagas were written, although there are certain indications within the sagas themselves that suggest that *Eirik's Saga* was written somewhere in the Breidafjord area (where the bulk of the Greenland settlers emigrated from) and that *Grænlendinga Saga* came from the north of Iceland, where Karlsefni and many of his descendants lived after his return from Vinland.

*

In the light of the literary circumstances which gave birth to these two sagas, it is hardly surprising that they should be so unsatisfactory as strictly historical sources. The authors were primarily interested in the people involved in the story of Vinland; they saw these explorations first and foremost as searching tests of character. Some people it matured, bringing to light new reserves of authority and resourcefulness, while others, like Freydis, it exposed: freed from the normal social pressures of a settled community her demanding nature erupted into cruel greed (*Grænlendinga Saga*, Chapter 8). Both sagas are full of fascinating character cameos whose rounded outlines are sketched with great economy but linger vividly in the memory: like Orm of Arnarstapi, the luckless mutual friend who was reluctantly persuaded to act as a marriage broker and died forlornly on a miserable voyage to Greenland (*Eirik's Saga*, Chapter 3), or like Thorbjorn Vifilsson, himself the son of a freed slave, haughtily rejecting the advances of the son of another freed slave, Einar of Thorgeirsfell (*Eirik's Saga*, Chapter 3).

Did they ever exist in this form, these people? There is, for instance, a generic similarity between the two eccentrics, Tyrkir the German in Leif's expedition (*Grænlendinga Saga*, Chapter 4) who got so wildly excited about finding grapes that he became incoherent, and Thorhall the Hunter in Karlsefni's expedition (*Eirik's Saga*, Chapter 8) who went off on his own to pray to his patron god, Thor. In the same way, the wife of Thorstein of Lysufjord changes from the formidable ogress Grimhild in *Grænlendinga Saga* (Chapter 6) into the much more agreeable Sigrid of *Eirik's Saga* (Chapter 6).

The literary genesis of the sagas, with their emphasis on character in action, helped to push cartography into the background. The details of how long the explorers sailed, or in what directions, are incidental; Vinland and the other areas of the North American coast are described only through the experience of the explorers themselves. The saga-writers were interested only in the aspects that interested the explorers – the natural resources (in comparison with the meagre fertility of Greenland), the harbourage, the grazing, the effect of weather on their husbandry. They noted the lush pastures, but what remained most vividly in the memory was the way that the beasts became frisky and difficult to manage when they were turned loose to graze on them (*Grænlendinga Saga*, Chapter 7). The explorers' reactions were subjective – the sweet taste of the dew of the New World after a long voyage across the North Atlantic; and the only apparent attempt at a scientific measurement of latitude (*Grænlendinga Saga*, Chapter 3) was more of an expression of wonder at the length of the shortest day in America, compared with Greenland or Iceland.

In addition to this, we have to recognize the possible extent of the tampering with the original texts that may have taken place. We know now that Hauk Erlendsson, in particular, altered many details, in some cases changing the actual sailing directions given in *Eirik's Saga* (Chapter 8). Did he have alternative sources of information? Or was he trying to improve the air of authenticity about them? Or was he deducing the directions from his own knowledge of cartography? It is impossible to be sure; but it must serve as a warning to anyone who hopes to read too much into the specific details given in the two sagas.

Some of the differences between the two sagas are deliberate, a conscious correcting of the one by the other. The author of *Eirik's Saga* had several motives, and the desire for objective truth was only one of them. It is hard to say how much he was influenced by a desire to show Gudrid and her family in as good a light as possible, how much by a natural literary determination to write a better saga. In the process, the differences between the sagas became more than those caused by the initial difficulty of reconciling the roles of Leif the Lucky.

But even when all this is said, we are still left with much of historical value in the sagas. There can be no doubt that the characters who play the leading roles in them actually existed; they are well-authenticated historical figures. There can be no doubt that they made journeys along the northern rim of the Atlantic and came upon a series of landfalls far to the west of the edge of European civilization. And there can be no doubt that the place where they attempted to found a Norse colony was somewhere along the Atlantic seaboard of the North American continent.

These three major, crucial facts cannot be reasonably disputed. Nor is there any need to dispute them. Obviously, specific details can become sadly distorted in the interval between occurrence and chronicling; but it is worth remembering that Ari the Learned, scrupulous historian that he was, testified that he had heard the story of Greenland from his uncle, who had got it from one of the original settlers – thus spanning the 140 years between 985 and 1125 with only one intermediary (see p. 26, above).

There were many ways in which traditions could survive the passing generations without undue distortion; and one of them was by means of incidental verses which were composed contemporaneously with the events concerned. These stanzas, with their intricate verse forms, were easier to remember than prose tales, and the stanzas that have been preserved in the Vinland Sagas are judged by many scholars to date from the early eleventh century (except for the Uniped stanza in *Eirik's Saga*, Chapter 12); they form a significant additional corroboration to the narrative told by the sagas.

The context in which the Vinland stanzas are now embedded may be hazy, but the general circumstantial impression is irresistible, despite the elusiveness of the information: a land lying south-west from Greenland, a long distance away, to the south of a country that is flat and stony and eventually glaciated; a land rich with grass and timber and wild wheat and wild grapes, abounding with game and fish, lovely in summer and mild in winter, somewhere to the south of the fiftieth parallel but no farther south than the southernmost haunt of the salmon in the Hudson River; a land inhabited by natives of related culture to the Inuit of Greenland and with habits strongly suggestive of Native American tribes. Take the general descriptions of shorelines and currents and havens as the Norsemen coasted down this seaboard. Relate all this to the *imago mundi* known to the medieval Icelandic geographers, and we can conclude that the Vinland of the saga-writers was envisaged as lying not very far from New England.

One intriguing question remains: did Christopher Columbus know of the Norsemen's exploits before he himself set off on his voyage across the Atlantic in 1492?

It is a tempting thought, especially as his son Fernando, in his biography of his father, quoted a note alleged to have been written by Columbus himself, which said, 'In the month of February in the year 1477 I sailed one hundred leagues beyond Tile Island.'

Tile Island (Thule) can presumably be equated with Iceland. But scholars have thrown doubt on the authenticity of this note and the trustworthiness of Columbus himself; and besides, it is strange that Columbus should have set course so far south if he had prior knowledge of certain land farther north. Even so, it could well be that stories about Vinland were current in the seaports of Europe in the fifteenth century, because throughout that period there was considerable, if illegal, trade between

Iceland and Bristol and between Bristol and Portugal; and certainly the Icelanders themselves had not forgotten about Vinland, or the general direction in which it lay. . . .

It is yet another tantalizing question mark in a story which leaves many questions as yet unanswered. Archaeology, textual studies, and cartographic investigation have all played their part in illuminating many of the enigmas of the Vinland story – and there is surely further illumination to come.

The story of Vinland is peripheral to the great body of Icelandic saga literature. But it is one of the most fascinating footnotes to the long history of the western world, and it is as such that we present these translations of the Vinland Sagas.

Scotland   MAGNUS MAGNUSSON
August, 1963   HERMANN PÁLSSON

November, 2003   M.M.

NOTE ON THE TRANSLATIONS (1965)

The translation of *Grænlendinga Saga* is based on the text in *Flateyjarbók*, edited by Matthias Þórðarson in *Íslenzk Fornrit*, vol. 4, Reykjavik, 1935.

The translation of *Eirik's Saga* is based on the text in *Skálholtsbók* (referred to as S), as reproduced by Sven B. F. Jansson in *Sagorna om Vinland*, vol. I, Lund, 1944. Certain variant readings from the text in *Hauksbók* (referred to as H), also reproduced by Professor Jansson, have been preferred without comment where the S text is obviously garbled or inferior; and the most important variants in H regarding Vinland are given in the footnotes.

We have relegated the saga-genealogies to the footnotes, where they do not impede the flow of the narrative. They (and the occasional variant readings) are printed in italics, to differentiate them from our own notes and comments, which we have tried to keep to a minimum.

There are two points of translation which require some comment here – the proper names, and the verses. There is no accepted standard for the treatment of Icelandic proper names, particularly place-names. Broadly speaking, our policy has been to leave uncompounded names in their Icelandic forms, but to translate or adapt wherever possible the topographical appellatives of compounded names – such as 'river', 'hill', 'dale', 'ness', 'fjord', 'tongue', 'heath', 'stead', '-by'.

We cannot lay claim to complete consistency; where consistency would have led us into absurdity or dissonance, we have preferred inconsistency. We have also dropped all accents, and transliterated the letters ð and þ into *d* and *th* respectively.

Personal nicknames have been translated wherever possible, but personal names have not been transliterated into English except that where people or places are well known under English names, we have abandoned the Icelandic forms.

NOTE ON TRANSLATIONS

Translation of the verses that stud many of the Old Icelandic sagas has always been a headache. After much experimentation, we have decided not to try to imitate the intricate verse-forms and the elaborate and resourceful poetic diction (*kennings*), but to retain as much as possible of their imagery in a free prose version. A literal translation is quite meaningless to the general reader, since there is no parallel in English to the skaldic convention of 'court-metre' with its intensely esoteric metaphor.

We have provided a List of Proper Names, to help the reader to sort out the relationship between the participants in the two sagas. There is also a Chronological Table to give historical perspective to the Vinland adventure. There is no Bibliography, because a very full account of all the publications on Vinland is available in *Islandica* (see p. 10, above). Many of the books that have been written about Vinland have been of value to us, and we would like to record here our grateful thanks to the host of scholars who have applied their learning to the unique problems presented by these two sagas. To have given individual acknowledgement to them all would have made this introduction impossibly unwieldy, and we have had to confine ourselves to citing only those works which have made the most decisive contributions to the scholarship of the subject.

We should like to thank the Librarian of the United States Information Service in London for allowing us prolonged access to material which was not readily available on this side of the Atlantic. And we owe a large debt of gratitude to Miss Bridget Gordon, B.A., B.Litt. (now Mrs Mackenzie) and Mr William Hook, B.Sc., both of whom made a painstaking scrutiny of this manuscript and contributed innumerable helpful suggestions.

M.M.
H.P.

GRÆNLENDINGA SAGA

I

Eirik explores Greenland

There was a man called Thorvald,[1] who was the father of Eirik the Red. He and Eirik left their home in Jaederen, in Norway, because of some killings and went to Iceland, which had been extensively settled by then; so to begin with they made their home at Drangar, in Hornstrands. Thorvald died there, and Eirik the Red then married Thjodhild[2] and moved south to make his home at Eirikstead, near Vatnshorn. They had a son called Leif.

Eirik was banished from Haukadale after killing Eyjolf Saur and Hrafn the Dueller, so he went west to Breidafjord and settled on Oxen Island, at Eirikstead. He lent his bench-boards[3] to Thorgest of Breidabolstead, but when he asked for them back they were not returned, which gave rise to quarrelling and fights between them, as *Eirik's Saga* describes.[4] Eirik was supported by Styr Thorgrimsson, Eyjolf of Svin Island, Thorbjorn Vifilsson, and the sons of Thorbrand of Alptafjord; Thorgest was supported by Thorgeir of Hitardale, and the sons of Thord Gellir.

Eirik was sentenced to outlawry at the Thorsness Assembly. He prepared his ship in Eiriksbay for a sea voyage, and when

1. *the son of Asvald, the son of Ulf, the son of Oxen-Thorir.*
2. *the daughter of Jorund Ulfsson and of Thorbjorg Ship-Breast, who was by then married to Thorbjorn of Haukadale.*
3. Bench-boards : presumably, carved decorative panels affixed to the front of the benches that ran down either side of the main room.
4. A very debatable reference : it can hardly refer to *Eirik's Saga* in its present form, because its account of Eirik's adventures in Iceland (Chapter 2) is very little fuller than here. This first chapter of *Grænlendinga Saga*, and the first two chapters of *Eirik's Saga*, are interpolations borrowed from *Landnámabók* (see pp. 31–2); many scholars believe that there must have been a lost *Eirik's Saga* which told the story of Eirik's life much more fully, and that the brief account in *Landnámabók* may well have been a condensed summary of it.

he was ready, Styr and the others accompanied him out beyond the islands. Eirik told them he was going to search for the land that Gunnbjorn, the son of Ulf Crow, had sighted when he was driven westwards off course and discovered the Gunnbjarnar Skerries;[1] he added that he would come back to visit his friends if he found this country.

He put out to sea past Snæfells Glacier. He found the country he was seeking and made land near the glacier he named Mid Glacier; it is now known as Blaserk.[2] From there he sailed south down the coast to find out if the country were habitable there. He spent the first winter on Eiriks Island, which lies near the middle of the Eastern Settlement. In the spring he went to Eiriksfjord, where he decided to make his home. That summer he explored the wilderness to the west and gave names to many landmarks there. He spent the second winter on Eiriks Holms, off Hvarfs Peak. The third summer he sailed all the way north to Snæfell and into Hrafnsfjord, where he reckoned he was farther inland than the head of Eiriksfjord. Then he turned back and spent the third winter on Eiriks Island, off the mouth of Eiriksfjord.

He sailed back to Iceland the following summer and put in at Breidafjord. He named the country he had discovered *Greenland*, for he said that people would be much more tempted to go there if it had an attractive name. Eirik spent the winter in Iceland. Next summer he set off to colonize Greenland, and he made his home at Brattahlid, in Eiriksfjord.

It is said by learned men[3] that in the summer in which Eirik the Red set off to colonize Greenland, twenty-five ships sailed

1. See p. 16 and List of Proper Names.
2. Eirik's course due west from Iceland to Greenland with a towering glacier as landmark at either end became the regular sailing route, and was in use until the fourteenth century, when increasing cold brought drift ice down from the Arctic and forced ships to take a more southerly course. Blaserk : for this and all other place-names, see List of Proper Names for the modern equivalents, where identifiable.
3. The 'learned men' are the twelfth-century historians of Iceland. This whole chapter is lifted from *Landnámabók* and substituted for the original saga-opening (see page 32).

from Breidafjord and Borgarfjord, but only fourteen reached there; some were driven back, and some were lost at sea. This was fifteen years before Christianity was adopted by law in Iceland, and in the same summer that Bishop Fridrek and Thorvald Kodransson went abroad.[1]

The following men who went abroad with Eirik took possession of land in Greenland : Herjolf Bardarson took possession of Herjolfsfjord, and made his home at Herjolfsness; Ketil took possession of Ketilsfjord; Hrafn, Hrafnsfjord; Solvi, Solvadale; Helgi Thorbrandsson, Alptafjord; Thorbjorn Glora, Siglufjord; Einar, Einarsfjord; Hafgrim, Hafgrimsfjord and Vatna District; and Arnlaug, Arnlaugsfjord. Others went to the Western Settlement.

2

Bjarni sights land to the west

Herjolf Bardarson[2] had lived for a time at Drepstokk; his wife was called Thorgerd, and they had a son called Bjarni.

Bjarni was a man of much promise. From early youth he had been eager to sail to foreign lands; he earned himself both wealth and a good reputation, and used to spend his winters alternately abroad and in Iceland with his father. He soon had a merchant ship of his own.

During the last winter that Bjarni spent in Norway, his father, Herjolf, sold up the farm and emigrated to Greenland with Eirik the Red. On board Herjolf's ship was a Christian from the

1. Either in 985 or 986. Iceland adopted Christianity in the year 1000 (cf. *Njal's Saga*, Chapters 100–5); and in *Íslendingabók*, Ari the Learned wrote that Greenland was settled fourteen or fifteen years before that date. Bishop Fridrek (from Germany) and Thorvald Kodransson (from the north of Iceland) were the first missionaries to make an organized attempt to convert Iceland. Their mission lasted for about five years (981–6), but ended abruptly when Thorvald killed two heathens who had lampooned him at the Althing; the missionaries then fled the country.

2. *He was the son of Bard, the son of Herjolf, a kinsman of Ingolf, the first settler of Iceland, who had given the family land between Vog and Reykjaness.*

Hebrides, the poet who composed the *Hafgerdinga Lay*;[1] this
was its refrain :

> I beseech the immaculate Master of monks
> To steer my journeys;
> May the Lord of the lofty heavens
> Hold his strong hand over me.

Herjolf made his home at Herjolfsness; he was a man of considerable stature.

Eirik the Red lived at Brattahlid. He commanded great respect, and all the people in Greenland recognized his authority.
He had three sons – Leif, Thorvald, and Thorstein. He also had
a daughter called Freydis, who was married to a man called
Thorvard; they lived at Gardar, where the bishop's residence
is now. Freydis was an arrogant, overbearing woman, but her
husband was rather feeble; she had been married off to him
mainly for his money.

Greenland was still a heathen country at this time.

Bjarni arrived in Iceland at Eyrar in the summer of the year
that his father had left for Greenland. The news came as a
shock to Bjarni, and he refused to have his ship unloaded. His
crew asked him what he had in mind; he replied that he intended to keep his custom of enjoying his father's hospitality
over the winter – 'so I want to sail my ship to Greenland, if
you are willing to come with me.'

They all replied that they would do what he thought best.
Then Bjarni said, 'This voyage of ours will be considered
foolhardy, for not one of us has ever sailed the Greenland
Sea.'

However, they put to sea as soon as they were ready and
sailed for three days until land was lost to sight below the
horizon. Then the fair wind failed and northerly winds and fog

---

1. Literally, 'Lay of the Breakers'. Only two more lines of this
poem have survived. It seems to have been written in connexion
with this voyage to Greenland. The term *hafgerðingar* refers to a
gross disturbance of the sea, probably submarine earthquakes, which
would account for the losses in the fleet.

set in, and for many days[1] they had no idea what their course was. After that they saw the sun again and were able to get their bearings; they hoisted sail and after a day's sailing they sighted land.[2]

They discussed amongst themselves what country this might be. Bjarni said he thought it could not be Greenland. The crew asked him if he wanted to land there or not; Bjarni replied, 'I think we should sail in close.'

They did so, and soon they could see that the country was not mountainous, but was well wooded and with low hills. So they put to sea again, leaving the land on the port quarter; and after sailing for two days they sighted land once more.

Bjarni's men asked him if he thought this was Greenland yet; he said he did not think this was Greenland, any more than the previous one – 'for there are said to be huge glaciers in Greenland.'

They closed the land quickly and saw that it was flat and wooded. Then the wind failed and the crew all said they thought it advisable to land there, but Bjarni refused. They claimed they needed both firewood and water; but Bjarni said, 'You have no shortage of either.' He was criticized for this by his men.

He ordered them to hoist sail, and they did so. They turned the prow out to sea and sailed before a south-west wind for three days before they sighted a third land. This one was high and mountainous, and topped by a glacier. Again they asked Bjarni if he wished to land there, but he replied, 'No, for this country seems to me to be worthless.'

They did not lower sail this time, but followed the coastline and saw that it was an island. Once again they put the land astern and sailed out to sea before the same fair wind. But now it began to blow a gale, and Bjarni ordered his men to shorten

1. *dœgr*: this term is ambiguous. Strictly speaking, it means 'day' in the sense of twelve hours, but it is also used in the sense of the astronomical 'day' of twenty-four hours, and there is often doubt about the particular meaning in many early texts.

2. Bjarni's landfall in the west cannot be identified with any certainty.

sail and not to go harder than ship and rigging could stand. They sailed now for four days, until they sighted a fourth land.

The men asked Bjarni if he thought this would be Greenland or not.

'This tallies most closely with what I have been told about Greenland,' replied Bjarni. 'And here we shall go in to land.'

They did so, and made land as dusk was falling at a promontory which had a boat hauled up on it. This was where Bjarni's father, Herjolf, lived, and it has been called Herjolfsness for that reason ever since.

Bjarni now gave up trading and stayed with his father, and carried on farming there after his father's death.

3

Leif explores Vinland

Some time later, Bjarni Herjolfsson sailed from Greenland to Norway and visited Earl Eirik,[1] who received him well. Bjarni told the earl about his voyage and the lands he had sighted. People thought he had shown great lack of curiosity, since he could tell them nothing about these countries, and he was criticized for this. Bjarni was made a retainer at the earl's court, and went back to Greenland the following summer.

There was now great talk of discovering new countries. Leif, the son of Eirik the Red of Brattahlid, went to see Bjarni Herjolfsson and bought his ship from him, and engaged a crew of thirty-five.

Leif asked his father Eirik to lead this expedition too, but Eirik was rather reluctant: he said he was getting old, and could endure hardships less easily than he used to. Leif replied that Eirik would still command more luck[2] than any of his kinsmen. And in the end, Eirik let Leif have his way.

As soon as they were ready, Eirik rode off to the ship which

1. Earl Eirik Hakonarson ruled over Norway from 1000 to 1014.
2. 'Luck' had a greater significance in pagan Iceland than the word implies now. Good luck or ill luck were innate qualities, part of the complex pattern of Fate. Leif inherited the good luck associated with his father (Chapter 4).

was only a short distance away. But the horse he was riding stumbled and he was thrown, injuring his leg.

'I am not meant to discover more countries than this one we now live in,' said Eirik. 'This is as far as we go together.'[1]

Eirik returned to Brattahlid, but Leif went aboard the ship with his crew of thirty-five. Among them was a Southerner called Tyrkir.[2]

They made their ship ready and put out to sea. The first landfall they made was the country that Bjarni had sighted last. They sailed right up to the shore and cast anchor, then lowered a boat and landed. There was no grass to be seen, and the hinterland was covered with great glaciers, and between glaciers and shore the land was like one great slab of rock. It seemed to them a worthless country.

Then Leif said, 'Now we have done better than Bjarni where this country is concerned – we at least have set foot on it. I shall give this country a name and call it *Helluland*.'[3]

They returned to their ship and put to sea, and sighted a second land. Once again they sailed right up to it and cast anchor, lowered a boat and went ashore. This country was flat and wooded, with white sandy beaches wherever they went; and the land sloped gently down to the sea.

Leif said, 'This country shall be named after its natural resources: it shall be called *Markland*.'[4]

They hurried back to their ship as quickly as possible and sailed away to sea in a north-east wind for two days until they sighted land again. They sailed towards it and came to an island which lay to the north of it.

They went ashore and looked about them. The weather was fine. There was dew on the grass, and the first thing they did was to get some of it on their hands and put it to their lips, and to them it seemed the sweetest thing they had ever tasted. Then

1. A fall from a horse was considered a very bad omen for a journey. Such a fall clinched Gunnar of Hlidarend's decision not to leave Iceland when he was outlawed (*Njal's Saga*, Chapter 75).

2. *Southerner* refers to someone from central or southern Europe; Tyrkir appears to have been a German.

3. Literally, 'Slab-land'; probably Baffin Island (see List of Names).

4. Literally, 'Forest-land'; probably Labrador (see List of Names).

they went back to their ship and sailed into the sound that lay between the island and the headland jutting out to the north.

They steered a westerly course round the headland. There were extensive shallows there and at low tide their ship was left high and dry, with the sea almost out of sight. But they were so impatient to land that they could not bear to wait for the rising tide to float the ship; they ran ashore to a place where a river flowed out of a lake. As soon as the tide had refloated the ship they took a boat and rowed out to it and brought it up the river into the lake, where they anchored it. They carried their hammocks ashore and put up booths.[1] Then they decided to winter there, and built some large houses.

There was no lack of salmon in the river or the lake, bigger salmon than they had ever seen.[2] The country seemed to them so kind that no winter fodder would be needed for livestock: there was never any frost all winter and the grass hardly withered at all.

In this country, night and day were of more even length than in either Greenland or Iceland: on the shortest day of the year, the sun was already up by 9 a.m., and did not set until after 3 p.m.[3]

When they had finished building their houses, Leif said to his companions, 'Now I want to divide our company into two parties and have the country explored; half of the company are to remain here at the houses while the other half go exploring – but they must not go so far that they cannot return the same evening, and they are not to become separated.'

They carried out these instructions for a time. Leif himself took turns at going out with the exploring party and staying behind at the base.

Leif was tall and strong and very impressive in appearance. He was a shrewd man and always moderate in his behaviour.

1. Booths were stone-and-turf enclosures which could be temporarily roofed with awnings for occupation.

2. On the east coast of the North American continent, salmon are not usually found any farther south than the Hudson River.

3. This statement indicates that the location of Vinland must have been south of latitude fifty and north of latitude forty – anywhere between the Gulf of St Lawrence and New Jersey.

4

Leif returns to Greenland

One evening news came that someone was missing: it was Tyrkir the Southerner. Leif was very displeased at this, for Tyrkir had been with the family for a long time, and when Leif was a child had been devoted to him. Leif rebuked his men severely, and got ready to make a search with twelve men.

They had gone only a short distance from the houses when Tyrkir came walking towards them, and they gave him a warm welcome. Leif quickly realized that Tyrkir was in excellent humour.

Tyrkir had a prominent forehead and shifty eyes, and not much more of a face besides; he was short and puny-looking but very clever with his hands.

Leif said to him, 'Why are you so late, foster-father? How did you get separated from your companions?'

At first Tyrkir spoke for a long time in German, rolling his eyes in all directions and pulling faces, and no one could understand what he was saying. After a while he spoke in Icelandic.

'I did not go much farther than you,' he said. 'I have some news. I found vines and grapes.'[1]

'Is that true, foster-father?' asked Leif.

'Of course it is true,' he replied. 'Where I was born there were plenty of vines and grapes.'

They slept for the rest of the night, and next morning Leif said to his men, 'Now we have two tasks on our hands. On alternate days we must gather grapes and cut vines, and then fell trees, to make a cargo for my ship.'

This was done. It is said that the tow-boat was filled with grapes. They took on a full cargo of timber; and in the spring

1. Many later explorers of the New England region commented on the wild grapes they found growing there. Grapes have been known to grow wild on the east coast as far north as Passama-quoddy Bay.

they made ready to leave and sailed away. Leif named the country after its natural qualities and called it *Vínland*.[1]

They put out to sea and had favourable winds all the way until they sighted Greenland and its ice-capped mountains. Then one of the crew spoke up and said to Leif, 'Why are you steering the ship so close to the wind?'

'I am keeping an eye on my steering,' replied Leif, 'but I am also keeping an eye on something else. Don't you see anything unusual?'

They said they could see nothing in particular.

'I am not quite sure,' said Leif, 'whether it is a ship or a reef I can see.'

Now they caught sight of it, and said that it was a reef. But Leif's eyesight was so much keener than theirs that he could now make out people on the reef.

'I want to sail close into the wind in order to reach these people,' he said. 'If they need our help, it is our duty to give it; but if they are hostile, then the advantages are all on our side and none on theirs.'

They approached the reef, lowered sail, anchored, and put out another small boat they had brought with them. Tyrkir asked the men who their leader was.

The leader replied that his name was Thorir, and that he was a Norwegian by birth. 'What is your name?' he asked.

Leif named himself in return.

'Are you a son of Eirik the Red of Brattahlid?'

Leif said that he was. 'And now,' he said, 'I want to invite

---

1. Literally, 'Wine-land'. With the compound *Vín-land*, compare the Icelandic term *vínber*, 'grapes' (literally, 'wine-berries'). In order to explain away the absence of grapes in certain parts of North America which have been suggested as the site of Vinland, some scholars (including Dr Helge Ingstad, cf. p. 9) have argued that the first element in the name is not *vín* ('wine') but *vin*, meaning 'fertile land', or 'oasis'. On phonological grounds this suggestion is nonsensical, since the name *Vínland* has never been forgotten in Iceland, and the words *vín* and *vin* are never confused. But the main objection is to be found in the sagas themselves, where the name of the country is explicitly associated with its wine.

you all aboard my ship, with as much of your belongings as the ship will take.'

They accepted the offer, and they all sailed to Eiriksfjord thus laden. When they reached Brattahlid they unloaded the ship.

Leif invited Thorir and his wife Gudrid and three other men to stay with him and found lodgings for the rest of the ship's company, both Thorir's men and his own crew.

Leif rescued fifteen people in all from the reef. From then on he was called Leif the Lucky. He gained greatly in wealth and reputation.

A serious disease broke out amongst Thorir's crew that winter and Thorir himself and many of his men died of it. Eirik the Red also died that winter.

Now there was much talk about Leif's Vinland voyage, and his brother Thorvald thought that the country had not been explored extensively enough.

Leif said to Thorvald, 'You can have my ship to go to Vinland, if you like; but first I want to send it to fetch the timber that Thorir left on the reef.'

This was done.

5
Thorvald explores Vinland

Thorvald prepared his expedition with his brother Leif's guidance and engaged a crew of thirty. When the ship was ready they put out to sea and there are no reports of their voyage until they reached Leif's Houses in Vinland. There they laid up the ship and settled down for the winter, catching fish for their food.

In the spring Thorvald said they should get the ship ready, and that meanwhile a small party of men should take the ship's boat and sail west along the coast and explore that region during the summer.

They found the country there very attractive, with woods stretching almost down to the shore and white sandy beaches.

There were numerous islands there, and extensive shallows. They found no traces of human habitation or animals except on one westerly island, where they found a wooden stack-cover. That was the only man-made thing they found; and in the autumn they returned to Leif's Houses.

Next summer Thorvald sailed east with his ship and then north along the coast. They ran into a fierce gale off a headland and were driven ashore; the keel was shattered and they had to stay there for a long time while they repaired the ship.

Thorvald said to his companions, 'I want to erect the old keel here on the headland, and call the place *Kjalarness*.'

They did this and then sailed away eastward along the coast. Soon they found themselves at the mouth of two fjords, and sailed up to the promontory that jutted out between them; it was heavily wooded. They moored the ship alongside and put out the gangway, and Thorvald went ashore with all his men.

'It is beautiful here,' he said. 'Here I should like to make my home.'

On their way back to the ship they noticed three humps on the sandy beach just in from the headland. When they went closer they found that these were three skin-boats,[1] with three men under each of them. Thorvald and his men divided forces and captured all of them except one, who escaped in his boat. They killed the other eight and returned to the headland, from which they scanned the surrounding country. They could make out a number of humps farther up the fjord and concluded that these were settlements.

Then they were overwhelmed by such a heavy drowsiness that they could not stay awake, and they all fell asleep – until they were awakened by a voice that shouted, 'Wake up, Thorvald, and all your men, if you want to stay alive! Get to your ship with all your company and get away as fast as you can!'

A great swarm of skin-boats was then heading towards them down the fjord.

Thorvald said, 'We shall set up breastworks on the gunwales

1. Certain Native American tribes of the New England area used canoes made of moose-hide instead of the more usual birch-bark.

and defend ourselves as best we can, but fight back as little as possible.'

They did this. The Skrælings[1] shot at them for a while, and then turned and fled as fast as they could.

Thorvald asked his men if any of them were wounded; they all replied that they were unhurt.

'I have a wound in the armpit,' said Thorvald. 'An arrow flew up between the gunwale and my shield, under my arm – here it is. This will lead to my death.

'I advise you now to go back as soon as you can. But first I want you to take me to the headland I thought so suitable for a home. I seem to have hit on the truth when I said that I would settle there for a while. Bury me there and put crosses at my head and feet, and let the place be called *Krossaness* for ever afterwards.'

(Greenland had been converted to Christianity by this time, but Eirik the Red had died before the conversion.)

With that Thorvald died, and his men did exactly as he had asked of them. Afterwards they sailed back and joined the rest of the expedition and exchanged all the news they had to tell.

They spent the winter there and gathered grapes and vines as cargo for the ship. In the spring they set off on the voyage to Greenland; they made land at Eiriksfjord, and had plenty of news to tell Leif.

6

Thorstein Eiriksson dies

Meanwhile, in Greenland, Thorstein Eiriksson of Eiriksfjord had married Gudrid Thorbjorn's-daughter, the widow of Thorir the Easterner, who was mentioned earlier.

Thorstein Eiriksson was now eager to go to Vinland to fetch

1. The term *Skræling* was used in early Icelandic sources to designate the inhabitants of Greenland and North America. The Skrælings of Vinland have been tentatively identified with the Micmac or extinct Beothuk Native American tribes. The derivation of the word is uncertain, but it has contemptuous associations – something like 'wretches'.

back the body of his brother Thorvald. He made the same ship ready and selected the biggest and strongest men available. He took a crew of twenty-five and his wife Gudrid as well.

When they were ready they put to sea and were soon out of sight of land. But throughout that summer they were at the mercy of the weather and never knew where they were going. Eventually, a week before winter, they made land at Lysufjord in the Western Settlement of Greenland. Thorstein looked for accommodation and found lodgings for all his crew, but he and his wife could find none, so the two of them stayed on board the ship for a few days.

At this time, Christianity was still in its infancy in Greenland.

Early one morning some people came to their tent, and their leader asked who was inside.

'Two people,' replied Thorstein. 'Who is asking?'

'My name is Thorstein,' said the other, 'and I am called Thorstein the Black. I have come here to invite you and your wife to come and stay with me.'

Thorstein Eiriksson replied that he wanted to consult his wife; but Gudrid left the decision to him and he accepted the invitation.

'Then I shall be back tomorrow with a cart to fetch you,' said Thorstein the Black. 'There is no lack of means to provide for you but you will find life at my house very dull, for there are only the two of us there, my wife and myself, and I am very unsociable. I am also of a different faith from yours, although I consider yours to be better than mine.'

Next morning he returned with a cart to fetch them. They moved over to his house to stay and were well looked after there.

Gudrid was a woman of striking appearance; she was very intelligent and knew well how to conduct herself amongst strangers.

Early that winter, disease broke out amongst Thorstein Eiriksson's crew and many of them died. Thorstein ordered coffins to be made for the dead and had the bodies laid out in the ship: 'For I want to have all their bodies brought to Eiriksfjord in the summer,' he said.

Not long afterwards the disease spread to Thorstein the Black's house and the first to fall ill was his wife, Grimhild. She was a huge woman, powerful as any man, but the disease laid her low just the same. Soon Thorstein Eiriksson caught the disease, and for a time the two of them were in bed ill, until Grimhild died. Her husband Thornstein the Black went outside to fetch a board on which to lay the corpse.

'Don't be too long, dear friend,' said Gudrid.

He said he would be back soon.

Then Thorstein Eiriksson said, 'There is something very odd about Grimhild. She is raising herself on her elbow and pushing her feet out of bed and groping for her shoes.'

At that moment Thorstein the Black returned to the room and Grimhild fell back on the bed so heavily that every beam in the house creaked.

Thorstein the Black made a coffin for Grimhild's body, laid her out, and took her away for burial. He was a big, powerful man, yet he needed all his strength to get her out of the house.

Thorstein Eiriksson's illness grew worse until he died. His wife Gudrid was grieved at his death. All three of them had been together in the room when he died, and Gudrid had been sitting on a stool beside her husband's bed. Now Thorstein the Black picked her up in his arms and sat down with her on his lap on the bench opposite her dead husband; he tried to comfort her and console her in every way he knew, and promised that he would take her to Eiriksfjord with her husband's body and the bodies of his crew.

'And I shall bring some more servants here,' he said, 'for your comfort and pleasure.'

She thanked him. Then the corpse of Thorstein Eiriksson suddenly sat up and said, 'Where is Gudrid?'

He said this three times, but Gudrid gave no answer. Then she said to Thorstein the Black, 'Should I answer him or not?'

He told her not to reply. Then he walked across the room and sat down on the stool with Gudrid on his knee and said, 'What is it you want, namesake?'

After a pause Thorstein Eiriksson replied, 'I am anxious to tell Gudrid her destiny, so that she may resign herself better to my death, for I have now come to a happy place of repose. I have this to say to you, Gudrid: you will marry an Icelander and you will have a long life together and your progeny will be great and vigorous, bright and excellent, sweet and fragrant. You and your husband will go from Greenland to Norway and from there to Iceland, where you will make your home and live for a long time. You will survive your husband and go on a pilgrimage to Rome, then return to your farm in Iceland; a church will be built there and you will be ordained a nun and stay there until you die.'

Then Thorstein fell back. His body was laid out and taken to the ship.

Thorstein the Black fulfilled all the promises he had made to Gudrid. In the spring he sold up his farm and livestock, took Gudrid and all her possessions to the ship, made the ship ready, engaged a crew, and then sailed to Eiriksfjord. All the dead were buried at the church there.

Gudrid went to stay with her brother-in-law Leif Eiriksson at Brattahlid. Thorstein the Black made his home in Eiriksfjord and lived there for the rest of his life. He was considered a man of great spirit.

7
Karlsefni in Vinland

That same summer a ship arrived in Greenland from Norway. Her captain was a man called Thorfinn Karlsefni.[1] He was a man of considerable wealth. He spent the winter with Leif Eiriksson at Brattahlid.

Karlsefni quickly fell in love with Gudrid and proposed to her, but she asked Leif to answer on her behalf. She was betrothed to Karlsefni, and the wedding took place that same winter.

There was still the same talk about Vinland voyages as before, and everyone, including Gudrid, kept urging Karlsefni to make

1. the son of Thord Horse-Head, the son of Snorri, the son of Thord of Hofdi.

the voyage. In the end he decided to sail and gathered a company of sixty men and five women. He made an agreement with his crew that everyone should share equally in whatever profits the expedition might yield. They took livestock of all kinds, for they intended to make a permanent settlement there if possible.

Karlsefni asked Leif if he could have the houses in Vinland; Leif said that he was willing to lend them, but not to give them away.

They put to sea and arrived safe and sound at Leif's Houses and carried their hammocks ashore. Soon they had plenty of good supplies, for a fine big rorqual was driven ashore; they went down and cut it up, and so there was no shortage of food.

The livestock were put out to grass, and soon the male beasts became very frisky and difficult to manage. They had brought a bull with them.

Karlsefni ordered timber to be felled and cut into lengths for a cargo for the ship, and it was left out on a rock to season. They made use of all the natural resources of the country that were available, grapes and game of all kinds and other produce.

The first winter passed into summer, and then they had their first encounter with Skrælings, when a great number of them came out of the wood one day. The cattle were grazing near by and the bull began to bellow and roar with great vehemence. This terrified the Skrælings and they fled, carrying their packs which contained furs and sables and pelts of all kinds. They made for Karlsefni's houses and tried to get inside, but Karlsefni had the doors barred against them. Neither side could understand the other's language.

Then the Skrælings put down their packs and opened them up and offered their contents, preferably in exchange for weapons; but Karlsefni forbade his men to sell arms. Then he hit on the idea of telling the women to carry milk out to the Skrælings, and when the Skrælings saw the milk they wanted to buy nothing else. And so the outcome of their trading expedition was that the Skrælings carried their purchases away in their bellies, and left their packs and furs with Karlsefni and his men.

After that, Karlsefni ordered a strong wooden palisade to be erected round the houses, and they settled in.

About this time Karlsefni's wife, Gudrid, gave birth to a son, and he was named Snorri.

Early next winter the Skrælings returned, in much greater numbers this time, bringing with them the same kind of wares as before. Karlsefni told the women, 'You must carry out to them the same produce that was most in demand last time, and nothing else.'

As soon as the Skrælings saw it they threw their packs in over the palisade.

Gudrid was sitting in the doorway beside the cradle of her son Snorri when a shadow fell across the door and a woman entered wearing a black, close-fitting tunic; she was rather short and had a band round her chestnut-coloured hair. She was pale, and had the largest eyes that have ever been seen in any human head. She walked up to Gudrid and said, 'What is your name?'

'My name is Gudrid. What is yours?'

'My name is Gudrid,' the woman replied.

Then Gudrid, Karlsefni's wife, motioned to the woman to come and sit beside her; but at that very moment she heard a great crash and the woman vanished, and in the same instant a Skræling was killed by one of Karlsefni's men for trying to steal some weapons. The Skrælings fled as fast as they could, leaving their clothing and wares behind. No one had seen the woman except Gudrid.

'Now we must devise a plan,' said Karlsefni, 'for I expect they will pay us a third visit, and this time with hostility and in greater numbers. This is what we must do: ten men are to go out on the headland here and make themselves conspicuous, and the rest of us are to go into the wood and make a clearing there, where we can keep our cattle when the Skrælings come out of the forest. We shall take our bull and keep him to the fore.'

The place where they intended to have their encounter with the Skrælings had the lake on one side and the woods on the other.

Karlsefni's plan was put into effect, and the Skrælings came right to the place that Karlsefni had chosen for the battle. The fighting began, and many of the Skrælings were killed. There was one tall and handsome man among the Skrælings and Karlsefni reckoned that he must be their leader. One of the Skrælings had picked up an axe, and after examining it for a moment he swung it at a man standing beside him, who fell dead at once. The tall man then took hold of the axe, looked at it for a moment, and then threw it as far as he could out into the water. Then the Skrælings fled into the forest as fast as they could, and that was the end of the encounter.

Karlsefni and his men spent the whole winter there, but in the spring he announced that he had no wish to stay there any longer and wanted to return to Greenland. They made ready for the voyage and took with them much valuable produce, vines and grapes and pelts. They put to sea and reached Eiriksfjord safely and spent the winter there.

8

Freydis in Vinland

Now there was renewed talk of voyaging to Vinland, for these expeditions were considered a good source of fame and fortune.

In the summer that Karlsefni returned from Vinland a ship arrived in Greenland from Norway, commanded by two brothers called Helgi and Finnbogi. They spent the winter in Greenland. They were Icelanders by birth and came from the Eastfjords.

One day, Freydis Eirik's-daughter travelled from her home at Gardar to visit the brothers Helgi and Finnbogi. She asked them if they would join her with their ship on an expedition to Vinland, sharing equally with her all the profits that might be made from it. They agreed to this. Then she went to see her brother Leif and asked him to give her the houses he had built in Vinland: but Leif gave the same answer as before – that he was willing to lend them but not to give them away.

The two brothers and Freydis had an agreement that each

party should have thirty able-bodied men on board, besides women. But Freydis broke the agreement at once by taking five more men, whom she concealed; and the brothers were unaware of this until they reached Vinland.

So they put to sea, and before they left they agreed to sail in convoy if possible. There was not much distance between them, but the brothers arrived in Vinland shortly before Freydis and had moved their cargo up to Leif's Houses by the time Freydis landed. Her crew unloaded her ship and carried the cargo up to the houses.

'Why have you put your stuff in here?' asked Freydis.

'Because,' the brothers replied, 'we had thought that the whole of our agreement would be honoured.'

'Leif lent these houses to me, not to you,' she said.

Then Helgi said, 'We brothers could never be a match for you in wickedness.'

They moved their possessions out and built themselves a house farther inland on the bank of a lake, and made themselves comfortable there. Meanwhile Freydis was having timber felled for her cargo.

When winter set in, the brothers suggested that they should start holding games and other entertainments. This was done for a while until trouble broke out and ill-feeling arose between the two parties. The games were abandoned and all visiting between the houses ceased; and this state of affairs continued for most of the winter.

Early one morning Freydis got up and dressed, but did not put on her shoes. There was heavy dew outside. She put on her husband's cloak and then walked to the door of the brothers' house. Someone had just gone outside, leaving the door ajar. She opened it and stood in the doorway for a while without a word. Finnbogi was lying in the bed farthest from the doorway; he was awake, and now he said, 'What do you want here, Freydis?'

'I want you to get up and come outside with me,' she replied. 'I want to talk to you.'

He did so, and they walked over to a tree-trunk that lay beside the wall of the house, and sat down on it.

'How are you getting on?' she asked.

'I like this good country,' he replied, 'but I dislike the ill-feeling that has arisen between us, for I can see no reason for it.'

'You are quite right,' she said, 'and I feel the same about it as you do. But the reason I came to see you is that I want to exchange ships with you and your brother, for your ship is larger than mine and I want to go away from here.'

'I shall agree to that,' he said, 'if that will make you happy.'

With that they parted. Finnbogi went back to his bed and Freydis walked home. When she climbed into bed her feet were cold and her husband Thorvard woke up and asked why she was so cold and wet. She answered with great indignation, 'I went over to see the brothers to offer to buy their ship, because I want a larger one; and this made them so angry that they struck me and handled me very roughly. But you, you wretch, would never avenge either my humiliation or your own. I realize now how far I am away from my home in Greenland! And unless you avenge this, I am going to divorce you.'[1]

He could bear her taunts no longer and told his men to get up at once and take their weapons. They did so, and went straight over to the brothers' house; they broke in while all the men were asleep, seized them and tied them up, and dragged them outside one by one. Freydis had each of them put to death as soon as he came out.

All the men were killed in this way, and soon only the women were left; but no one was willing to kill them.

Freydis said, 'Give me an axe.'

This was done, and she herself killed the women, all five of them.

After this monstrous deed they went back to their house, and it was obvious that Freydis thought she had been very clever about it. She said to her companions, 'If we ever manage to get back to Greenland I shall have anyone killed who breathes a

1. Under Icelandic law of this period, a woman had equal rights in marriage and could obtain a divorce by declaration. If she were judged to have valid grounds she could claim half of the husband's estate.

word about what has just happened. Our story will be that these people stayed on here when we left.'

Early in the spring they prepared the ship that had belonged to the brothers and loaded it with all the produce they could get and the ship could carry. Then they put to sea. They had a good voyage and reached Eiriksfjord early in the summer.

Karlsefni was still there when they arrived. His ship was all ready to sail and he was only waiting for a favourable wind. It is said that no ship has ever sailed from Greenland more richly laden than the one Karlsefni commanded.

9
Karlsefni's descendants

Freydis returned to her farm, which had in no way suffered during her absence. She loaded all her companions with money, for she wanted them to keep her crimes secret; and then she settled down on her farm.

But her companions were not all discreet enough to say nothing about these evil crimes and prevent them from becoming known. Eventually word reached the ears of her brother Leif, who thought it a hideous story. He seized three of Freydis' men and tortured them into revealing everything that had happened; their stories tallied exactly.

'I do not have the heart,' said Leif, 'to punish my sister Freydis as she deserves. But I prophesy that her descendants will never prosper.'

And after that no one thought anything but ill of her and her family.

Meanwhile Karlsefni had prepared his ship and sailed away. He had a good voyage and reached Norway safe and sound. He spent the winter there and sold his cargo, and he and his wife were made much of by the noblest in the country. Next spring he prepared his ship for the voyage to Iceland; when he was quite ready to sail and his ship lay waiting at the wharf for a favourable wind, a Southerner came to see him – a man from Bremen, in Saxony.

This man asked Karlsefni if he were willing to sell the carved gable-head[1] he had on the ship.

'I do not want to sell it,' replied Karlsefni.

'I shall give you half a mark of gold for it,' said the Southerner.

Karlsefni thought this a good offer; the bargain was struck and the Southerner went away with the carved gable-head. Karlsefni did not know what kind of wood it was made from: it was maple,[2] and had come from Vinland.[3]

Karlsefni put to sea and reached the north of Iceland, making land in Skagafjord where he laid up his ship for the winter. Next spring he bought the lands at Glaumby and made his home there; he farmed there for the rest of his life, and was considered a man of great stature. Many people of high standing are descended from him and his wife Gudrid.

After Karlsefni's death Gudrid and her son Snorri, who had been born in Vinland, took over the farm. When Snorri married, Gudrid went abroad on a pilgrimage to Rome; when she returned to her son's farm he had built a church at Glaumby. After that Gudrid became a nun and stayed there as an anchoress for the rest of her life.

Snorri had a son called Thorgeir, who was the father of Yngvild, the mother of Bishop Brand.[4] Snorri also had a daughter called Hallfrid, who was the wife of Runolf, the father of Bishop Thorlak.[5]

1. *Húsasnotra*: decorative carving chiefly used on the gables of houses, but also on ships.

2. *Mosuri*: usually translated 'maple'. But the word was probably applied to a variety of trees.

3. Typical of the elliptical style of the sagas. The gable-head which so attracted the Southerner from Bremen must surely have been a work of art carved by his fellow-Southerner Tyrkir, who was said to be such a good craftsman, 'very clever with his hands' (Chapter 4).

4. Bishop Brand Sæmundarson: bishop of Holar, in the north of Iceland, 1163–1201.

5. Bishop Thorlak Runolfsson: bishop of Skalholt, in the south of Iceland, 1118–33. He was one of the two bishops for whom Ari the Learned wrote *Íslendingabók*, the earliest vernacular history of Iceland (see p. 26).

Karlsefni and Gudrid had another son, who was called Bjorn; he was the father of Thorunn, the mother of Bishop Bjorn.[1]

A great many people are descended from Karlsefni; he has become the ancestor of a prolific line.

It was Karlsefni himself who told more fully than anyone else the story of all these voyages, which has been to some extent recorded here.

1. Bishop Bjorn Gilsson : bishop of Holar, 1147–62.

EIRIK'S SAGA

I

Gudrid's ancestry

There was a warrior king called Olaf the White, who was the son of King Ingjald.[1] Olaf went on a Viking expedition to the British Isles, where he conquered Dublin and the adjoining territory and made himself king over them. He married Aud the Deep-Minded, the daughter of Ketil Flat-Nose;[2] they had a son called Thorstein the Red.

Olaf was killed in battle in Ireland, and Aud and Torstein the Red then went to the Hebrides. There Thorstein married Thurid, the daughter of Eyvind the Easterner;[3] they had many children.

Thorstein the Red became a warrior king, and joined forces with Earl Sigurd the Powerful;[4] together they conquered Caithness, Sutherland, Ross, and Moray, and more than half of Argyll. Thorstein ruled over these territories as king until he was betrayed by the Scots and killed in battle.

Aud the Deep-Minded was in Caithness when she learned of Thorstein's death; she had a ship built secretly in a forest, and when it was ready she sailed away to Orkney. There she gave away in marriage Groa, daughter of Thorstein the Red.[5]

After that, Aud set out for Iceland; she had twenty freeborn men aboard her ship. She reached Iceland and spent the first winter with her brother Bjorn at Bjarnarhaven. Then she took possession of the entire Dales district between Dogurdar River and Skraumuhlaups River, and made her home at Hvamm. She used to say prayers at Kross Hills; she had crosses erected there, for she had been baptized and was a devout Christian.

Many well-born men, who had been taken captive in the

1. *the son of Helgi, the son of Olaf, the son of Gudrod, the son of Halfdan White-Leg, king of the Uplanders.*
2. *the son of Bjorn Buna, an excellent man in Norway.*
3. *and the sister of Helgi the Lean.*
4. *the son of Eystein the Noisy.*
5. *Groa's daughter was Grelod, who married Earl Thorfinn the Skull-Splitter* (earl of Orkney, d. 963).

British Isles by Vikings and were now slaves, came to Iceland with her. One of them was called Vifil; he was of noble descent. He had been taken prisoner in the British Isles and was a slave until Aud gave him his freedom.

When Aud gave land to members of her crew, Vifil asked her why she did not give him some land like the others. Aud replied that it was of no importance, and said that he would be considered a man of quality wherever he was. She gave him Vifilsdale, and he settled there. He married, and had two sons called Thorbjorn and Thorgeir; they were both promising men, and grew up with their father.

2

Eirik explores Greenland

There was a man called Thorvald,[1] who was the father of Eirik the Red. He and Eirik left their home in Jaederen because of some killings and went to Iceland. They took possession of land in Hornstrands, and made their home at Drangar. Thorvald died there, and Eirik the Red then married Thjodhild,[2] and moved south to Haukadale; he cleared land there and made his home at Eirikstead, near Vatnshorn.

Eirik's slaves started a landslide that destroyed the farm of a man called Valthjof, at Valthjofstead; so Eyjolf Saur, one of Valthjof's kinsmen, killed the slaves at Skeidsbrekkur, above Vatnshorn. For this, Eirik killed Eyjolf Saur; he also killed Hrafn the Dueller, at Leikskalar. Geirstein and Odd of Jorvi, who were Eyjolf's kinsmen, took action over his killing, and Eirik was banished from Haukadale.

Eirik then took possession of Brok Island and Oxen Island, and spent the first winter at Tradir, in South Island. He lent his bench-boards to Thorgest of Breidabolstead. After that, Eirik moved to Oxen Island, and made his home at Eirikstead. He then asked for his bench-boards back, but they were not re-

1. *the son of Asvald, the son of Ulf, the son of Oxen-Thorir.*
2. *the daughter of Jorund Ulfsson and of Thorbjorg Ship-Breast, who was by then married to Thorbjorn of Haukadale.*

turned; so Eirik went to Breidabolstead and seized them. Thorgest pursued him, and they fought a battle near the farmstead at Drangar. Two of Thorgest's sons and several other men were killed there.

After this, both Eirik and Thorgest maintained a force of fighting-men at home. Eirik was supported by Styr Thorgrimsson, Eyjolf of Svin Island, Thorbjorn Vifilsson, and the sons of Thorbrand of Alptafjord; Thorgest was supported by Thorgeir of Hitardale, Aslak of Langadale and his son Illugi, and the sons of Thord Gellir.

Eirik and his men were sentenced to outlawry at the Thorsness Assembly. He made his ship ready in Eiriksbay, and Eyjolf of Svin Island hid him in Dimunarbay while Thorgest and his men were scouring the islands for him.

Thorbjorn Vifilsson and Styr and Eyjolf accompanied Eirik out beyond the islands, and they parted in great friendship; Eirik said he would return their help as far as it lay within his power, if ever they had need of it. He told them he was going to search for the land that Gunnbjorn, the son of Ulf Crow, had sighted when he was driven westwards off course and discovered the Gunnbjarnar Skerries; he added that he would come back to visit his friends if he found this country.

Eirik put out to sea past Snæfells Glacier, and made land near the glacier that is known as Blaserk. From there he sailed south to find out if the country were habitable there. He spent the first winter on Eiriks Island, which lies near the middle of the Eastern Settlement. In the spring he went to Eiriksfjord, where he decided to make his home. That summer he explored the wilderness to the west and gave names to many landmarks there. He spent the second winter on Eiriks Holms, off Hvarfs Peak. The third summer he sailed all the way north to Snæfell and into Hrafnsfjord, where he reckoned he was farther inland than the head of Eiriksfjord. Then he turned back and spent the third winter on Eiriks Island, off the mouth of Eiriksfjord.

He sailed back to Iceland the following summer and put in at Breidafjord. He stayed the winter with Ingolf of Holmlatur. In the spring he fought a battle with Thorgest of Breidabolstead and was defeated. After that a reconciliation was arranged between them.

That summer Eirik set off to colonize the country he had discovered; he named it *Greenland*, for he said that people would be much more tempted to go there if it had an attractive name.

3

Gudrid goes to Greenland

Thorgeir Vifilsson married Arnora, the daughter of Einar of Laugarbrekka.[1]

Thorbjorn Vifilsson married another of Einar's daughters, called Hallveig, and thereby acquired some land at Hellisvellir, in Laugarbrekka, and moved house there. Thorbjorn became a man of considerable stature; he was a chieftain[2] and ran a large farm. He had a daughter called Gudrid, who was very beautiful and a most exceptional woman in every respect.

A man called Orm lived at Arnarstapi; he had a wife called Halldis. Orm was a good farmer. He and Thorbjorn Vifilsson were great friends, and Gudrid lived at Arnarstapi with Orm as his foster-daughter for a long time.

There was a man called Thorgeir, who lived at Thorgeirsfell; he was a freed slave, and was now a very wealthy man. He had a son called Einar, who was a handsome and courteous man with a taste for the ornate; Einar was a successful sea-going trader, and used to spend his winters alternately in Iceland and in Norway.

It so happened one autumn when Einar was in Iceland that he made a trading trip out along Snæfellsness with his goods and came to Arnarstapi, where Orm invited him to stay; Einar

1. *the son of Sigmund, the son of Ketil Thistle, who had settled Thistilsfjord.*

2. *Goðorðsmaðr*; in the medieval republic of Ireland (see p. 13), authority was invested in the priest-chieftains (there were thirty-nine at this time), whose functions were both religious and secular. The *goðorð* was an hereditary office, but it could be disposed of in a number of ways – divided, sold, and even lent.

accepted, for they were on friendly terms. His goods were taken into an outhouse.

Einar opened his bales and showed them to Orm and his household, and invited Orm to have anything from them he wished. Orm accepted the offer, and called Einar a trader of of distinction and a man of great good fortune. As they were examining the wares a woman passed the doorway. Einar asked Orm who the beautiful woman was who had just passed in front of the door – 'I have never seen her here before.'

'That is my foster-daughter, Gudrid,' replied Orm, 'the daughter of Thorbjorn of Laugarbrekka.'

'She must be an excellent match,' said Einar. 'I suppose there have been some suitors after her hand?'

'There have certainly been suitors, my friend,' replied Orm, 'but her hand is not to be had for the asking. She is obviously rather particular about husbands, and so is her father.'

'Be that as it may,' said Einar, 'she is the woman whose hand I intend to seek, and I would like you to broach the matter with her father on my behalf and do your utmost in urging it; I shall repay you with my firmest friendship. Thorbjorn should realize that such a family alliance would suit both of us very well; he is a man of great standing and has an excellent farm, but I hear that his money is dwindling fast; whereas I am short of neither land nor money, nor is my father. And so it would be a great asset for Thorbjorn if the marriage were to take place.'

'I certainly consider myself your friend,' said Orm, 'but even so I am rather reluctant to raise this matter, for Thorbjorn is a proud man, and a very ambitious one too.'

Einar insisted on the marriage proposal being made, and Orm agreed to let him have his way. Einar then travelled back south to his home.

A little later Thorbjorn held an autumn feast as was his custom, for he was a man of large generosity. Orm of Arnarstapi was present, along with many others of Thorbjorn's friends. Orm had a word with Thorbjorn and told him that Einar of Thorgeirsfell had been visiting him recently, and was proving to be a promising young man; and then Orm made the marriage proposal on Einar's behalf, and said that the match would be a very suitable one for a number of reasons: 'It could be a great asset to you, Thorbjorn, because of the money involved,' he said.

Thorbjorn replied, 'I never expected to hear such a suggestion from you – that I should marry my daughter to the son of a slave! My lack of money must be very obvious to you! And since you thought her worthy of such a meagre match, she shall not go back with you to your home.'

Orm and all the other guests went home; but Gudrid remained behind and stayed with her father that winter.

In the spring Thorbjorn again held a lavish feast for his friends; there were many people present, and the feast went very well. During it Thorbjorn asked for a hearing, and said, 'I have spent a long life here; I have enjoyed the favour and friendship of others, and I can say that we have always got on well together.

'But now I find myself in financial difficulties. This home of mine has hitherto never been considered a humble one, and I would now rather abandon my farm than forfeit my dignity, rather leave the country than disgrace my kinsmen. I have decided to take up the offer that my friend Eirik the Red made to me when we took leave of one another in Breidafjord; I intend to go to Greenland this summer, if I can have my way.'

This decision came as a shock to everyone, for Thorbjorn had always been well liked. But they realized that since he had announced it like this there would be no point in trying to dissuade him.

After that, Thorbjorn gave gifts to his guests; the feast was over, and everyone went back home.

Thorbjorn sold up his lands and bought a ship which was lying in Hraunhafnar Estuary. Thirty people decided to go with him to Greenland; among them were Orm of Arnarstapi and his wife, and others of Thorbjorn's friends who did not want to part from him.

They set sail and had good weather to start with, but when they reached open sea the favourable wind failed them; they ran into severe storms and could make little headway all summer. Then disease broke out on board and half the crew, including Orm and his wife Halldis, died. The seas worsened, and they suffered terribly from exposure and other hardships. Finally they made land at Herjolfsness, right at the beginning of winter.

The farmer at Herjolfsness was a capable and worthy man called Thorkel.[1] He invited Thorbjorn and all his crew to stay for the whole winter, and treated them with great hospitality. Thorbjorn and all his crew liked it there.

4

Gudrid is told her future

At that time there was severe famine in Greenland. Those who had gone out on hunting expeditions had had little success, and some had never come back.

There was a woman in the settlement who was called Thorbjorg; she was a prophetess, and was known as the Little Sybil. She had had nine sisters,[2] but she was the only one left alive. It was her custom in winter to attend feasts; she was always invited, in particular, by those who were most curious about their own fortunes or the season's prospects. Since Thorkel of Herjolfsness was the chief farmer in the district, it was thought to be his responsibility to find out when the current hardships would come to an end.

Thorkel invited the prophetess to his house and prepared a good reception for her, as was the custom when such women were being received. A high-seat was made ready for her with a cushion on it, which had to be stuffed with hens' feathers.

She arrived in the evening with the man who had been sent to escort her. She was dressed like this: she wore a blue mantle fastened with straps and adorned with stones all the way down

1. According to *Landnámabók* the farmer at Herjolfsness at this time was Herjolf Bardarson. *Grœnlendinga Saga* (Chapter 2) describes Herjolf's emigration from Iceland to Greenland, and says that his son Bjarni farmed at Herjolfsness afterwards.

2. H adds: *and they had all been prophetesses.*

to the hem. She had a necklace of glass beads. On her head she wore a black lambskin hood lined with white cat's-fur. She carried a staff with a brass-bound knob studded with stones. She wore a belt made of touchwood, from which hung a large pouch, and in this she kept the charms she needed for her witchcraft. On her feet were hairy calfskin shoes with long thick laces which had large tin buttons on the ends. She wore catskin gloves, with the white fur inside.

When she entered the room everyone felt obliged to proffer respectful greetings, to which she responded according to her opinion of each person. Thorkel took her by the hand and led her to the seat which had been prepared for her. He asked her to cast her eyes over his home and household and herds; she had little to say about anything.

Later that evening the tables were set up; and this is what the prophetess had for her meal: she was given a gruel made from goat's milk, and a main dish of hearts from the various kinds of animals that were available there. She used a brass spoon, and a knife with a walrus-tusk handle bound with two rings of copper; the blade had a broken point.

When the tables had been removed, Thorkel went over to Thorbjorg and asked her how she liked his home and people's behaviour there, and how soon she would know the answer to his question which everyone wanted to learn. She replied that she would not give any answer until the following morning, when she had slept there overnight first.

Late next day she was supplied with the preparations she required for performing the witchcraft. She asked for the assistance of women who knew the spells needed for performing the witchcraft, known as Warlock-songs; but there were no such women available. So inquiries were then made amongst all the people on the farm, to see if anyone knew the songs.

Then Gudrid said, 'I am neither a sorceress nor a witch, but when I was in Iceland my foster-mother Halldis taught me spells which she called Warlock-songs.'

Thorbjorg said, 'Then your knowledge is timely.'

'This is the sort of knowledge and ceremony that I want nothing to do with,' said Gudrid, 'for I am a Christian.'

'It may well be,' said Thorbjorg, 'that you could be of help to others over this, and not be any the worse a woman for that. But I shall leave it to Thorkel to provide whatever is required.'

So Thorkel now brought pressure on Gudrid, and she consented to do as he wished.

The women formed a circle round the ritual platform on which Thorbjorg seated herself. Then Gudrid sang the songs so well and beautifully that those present were sure they had never heard lovelier singing. The prophetess thanked her for the song.

'Many spirits are now present,' she said, 'which were charmed to hear the singing, and which previously had tried to shun us and would grant us no obedience. And now many things stand revealed to me which before were hidden both from me and from others.

'I can now say that this famine will not last much longer, and that conditions will improve with the spring; and the epidemic which has persisted for so long will abate sooner than expected.

'And as for you, Gudrid, I shall reward you at once for the help you have given us, for I can see your whole destiny with great clarity now. You will make a most distinguished marriage here in Greenland, but it will not last for long, for your paths all lead to Iceland; there you will start a great and eminent family line, and over your progeny there shall shine a bright light. And now farewell, my daughter.'

Then everyone went over to the prophetess, each asking her whatever he was most curious to know. She answered them readily, and there were few things that did not turn out as she prophesied.

After this a messenger arrived for her from a neighbouring farm and she went there with him. Then Thorbjorn was sent for; he had refused to remain in the house while such pagan practices were being performed.

The weather quickly improved as spring approached, just as Thorbjorg had foretold. Thorbjorn made his ship ready and sailed off to Brattahlid, where Eirik the Red welcomed him with open arms and said that it was good to have him there. Thorbjorn and his family stayed with Eirik the following winter.

Next spring Eirik gave Thorbjorn land at Stokkaness; Thorbjorn built a good house there, and lived there from then on.

5

Leif discovers Vinland

Eirik was married to a woman called Thjodhild, and had two sons,[1] Thorstein and Leif; they were both promising young men. Thorstein stayed at home with his father, and no one in Greenland at that time was considered so promising.

Leif had sailed to Norway, where he stayed with King Olaf Tryggvason. But when he had set sail from Greenland in the summer, his ship was driven off course to the Hebrides. He and his men stayed most of the summer there while they were waiting for favourable winds.

Leif fell in love there with a woman called Thorgunna; she was of noble birth, and Leif came to realize that she was a woman of unusual knowledge. When he was about to depart, Thorgunna asked if she could go with him. Leif asked if her kinsmen approved of that; she said she did not care. Leif said he did not think it advisable for him to abduct so well-born a woman in a foreign country – 'for there are so few of us.'

'I am not sure that you will prefer the alternative,' said Thorgunna.

'I shall take that risk,' replied Leif.

'Then I must tell you,' said Thorgunna, 'that I am with child, and that you are responsible for the baby I am expecting. I have a premonition that I shall give birth to a son when the time comes; and even though you refuse to let it concern you, I intend to bring the boy up and send him to you in Greenland as soon as he can travel with others. I have the feeling that you will not enjoy having a son by me any more than our

1. H adds: *by her*. Cf. Chapters 8 and 12, where a third son, Thorvald, is mentioned; he was perhaps illegitimate, like Freydis (Chapter 8, p. 93, note 5).

parting now warrants; and I intend to come to Greenland myself in the end.'

Leif gave her a gold ring and a Greenland mantle of home-spun cloth and a belt of walrus ivory.

The boy, who was named Thorgils, later arrived in Greenland, and Leif acknowledged him as his son; according to some people this Thorgils came to Iceland the summer before the Frodriver Marvels.[1] Thorgils then went to Greenland, and there seemed to be something uncanny about him all his life.

Leif and his men sailed from the Hebrides and reached Norway in the autumn. He joined the court of King Olaf Tryggvason, who bestowed great honour on him and thought him a very accomplished man.

On one occasion the king had a talk with Leif and said, 'Are you intending to sail to Greenland this summer?'

'Yes,' replied Leif, 'if you approve.'

'I think it would be a good idea,' said the king. 'You are to go there with a mission from me, to preach Christianity in Greenland.'

Leif said that it was for the king to command, but added that in his opinion this mission would be difficult to accomplish in Greenland. The king replied that he could think of no one better fitted for it than him – 'and your good luck will see you through.'

'That will only be,' replied Leif, 'if I have the benefit of yours too.'

Leif set sail when he was ready; he ran into prolonged difficulties at sea, and finally came upon lands whose existence

1. These supernatural events, which took place in 1000–1, are most dramatically described in *Eyrbyggja Saga*, Chapters 50–5. A 'Hebridean woman called Thorgunna', skilled in magic, came to the farm at Frodriver, in Snæfellsness; and after her death there was a grim series of hauntings, apparitions, omens, and tragic deaths, before the evil was exorcized.

This reference in *Eirik's Saga* is incompatible with the *Eyrbyggja Saga* account. Leif's alleged mission to Greenland would have taken place in 1000, if it is to be reconciled with other Icelandic sources; but the Thorgunna of *Eyrbyggja Saga* was said to be in her fifties when she came to Frodriver in that year.

he had never suspected. There were fields of wild wheat grow-ing there,[1] and vines, and among the trees there were maples. They took some samples of all these things.[2]

Leif came across some shipwrecked seamen and brought them home with him and gave them all hospitality throughout the winter. He showed his great magnanimity and goodness by bringing Christianity to the country and by rescuing these men; he was known as Leif the Lucky.

He made land at Eiriksfjord and went home to Brattahlid, where he was given a good welcome. He at once began preach-ing Christianity and the Catholic faith throughout the country; he revealed to the people King Olaf Tryggvason's message, telling them what excellence and what glory there was in this faith.

Eirik was reluctant to abandon his old religion; but his wife, Thjodhild, was converted at once, and she had a church built not too close to the farmstead. This building was called Thjod-hild's Church, and there she and the many others who had accepted Christianity would offer up their prayers. Thjodhild refused to live with Eirik after she was converted, and this annoyed him greatly.[3]

1. Literally 'self-sown wheat': usually identified with wild rice (*zizania aquatica*), which grows as far north as Newfoundland and was commented upon by later explorers, such as Jacques Cartier in 1534, who made special mention of the 'fields of wild corn'.

2. H adds: *some of the trees were so large that they were used for house-building*. All the details mentioned here are consistent with a landfall somewhere in the New England region. Cf. also the notes on wild grapes and maple trees in *Grænlendinga Saga*, Chap-ters 4 and 9.

3. Eirik the Red's farmstead at Brattahlid (now Kagssiarssuk) was meticulously excavated by the National Museum of Denmark in 1932, revealing a large complex of buildings of Norse design. But no trace of 'Thjodhild's Church' was found – a negative fact that tended to discredit this section of the saga. But in August 1961 a workman digging foundations for a school-hostel at Kagssiarssuk came across a human skull, which was soon pronounced to be that of a medieval Norseman. The following summer, in 1962, full-scale excavations were carried out which revealed the foundations of a tiny medieval church, only sixteen feet long by eight feet in area,

There was now much talk of going to search for this country that Leif had discovered. The leader in this was his brother, Thorstein Eiriksson, a well-informed and popular man. Eirik the Red was also approached, for people had great faith in his good luck and foresight. He was reluctant at first, but did not refuse when his friends urged him.

The ship that Thorbjorn Vifilsson had brought from Iceland was now made ready, and twenty men were engaged for the voyage. They took with them little in the way of livestock, but mainly weapons and provisions.

On the morning that Eirik left home for the ship he took a chest full of gold and silver and hid it. Then he rode on his way; but before he had gone very far he was thrown from his horse, breaking some ribs and injuring his shoulder, and cried out 'A-aah!' As a result he sent a message to his wife telling her to remove the treasure he had hidden : he said that he had been punished for hiding it.[1]

Then they sailed out of Eiriksfjord. They were in high spirits and were pleased with their prospects. But they ran into prolonged difficulties and were unable to reach the seas they wanted. At one time they were within sight of Iceland; at another they observed birds off Ireland. Their ship was driven back and forth across the ocean. In the autumn they turned back towards Greenland and reached Eiriksfjord at the beginning of winter, worn out by exposure and toil.

with four-foot-thick walls of turf and timber, set inside a small churchyard containing some eighty graves. The church stood some 200 yards from Eirik's home, and was concealed from it by a fold in the rising ground.

The other medieval Norse churches discovered in Greenland were all built of stone. This very primitive and humble turf church can only be identified with 'Thjodhild's Church', which was built 'not too close to the farmstead' of Brattahlid. This does not, of course, prove that it was Leif who brought Christianity to Greenland; there are compelling reasons for believing that Leif's mission never took place at all (see pp. 32–3).

1. The burying of money was illegal in Christian Iceland.

Then Eirik said, 'You[1] were much more cheerful in the summer when you[1] were sailing out of the fjord than we are now; but there are still many good things in store for us.'

Thorstein replied, 'It would be a noble gesture to provide for all those who are now without resources, and find them lodgings for the winter.'

'There is much truth in the saying that one never knows until one is answered,' said Eirik. 'And so it is now. What you suggest shall be done.'

All those who had nowhere to stay went ashore and went home with Eirik and his son.

6

Thorstein Eiriksson dies

It so happened that Thorstein Eiriksson asked for the hand of Gudrid Thorbjorn's-daughter; the proposal was well received, both by Gudrid and her father. Agreement was reached, and Thorstein married Gudrid. The wedding took place at Brattahlid in the autumn; the wedding-feast was well attended and was a great success.

Thorstein had a farm at Lysufjord, in the Western Settlement. Another man, also called Thorstein, was joint-owner of the farm; his wife was called Sigrid.

Thorstein Eiriksson moved to Lysufjord in the autumn with his wife Gudrid to stay with his namesake, and they were well received there. They settled there for the winter.

Early in the winter, disease broke out at the farm. The overseer of the farm, an unpopular man called Gardi, was the first to be taken ill and die. In a short time many others had caught the disease, and died one after another. Then Thorstein Eiriksson and Sigrid, the wife of his namesake, fell ill.

One evening Sigrid wanted to go outside to the privy that

---

1. H – *we*. The reading in S suggests that Eirik never went on this expedition. Cf. *Grænlendinga Saga*, Chapter 3, where the fall from his horse makes Eirik decide to stay at home.

was opposite the main door. Gudrid went with her. While they were outside, facing the door, Sigrid cried out, 'Oh!'

Gudrid said, 'We are being very careless; you should not have come out into the cold. We must hurry back inside.'

'I am not going in now,' said Sigrid, 'for all the dead are lined up before the door. I can see your husband Thorstein amongst them, and I can also see myself there. What a horrible sight!'

But it passed off, and she said, 'I cannot see them now.'

The dead overseer, who had seemed to her to be trying to flog the others with a whip, had also vanished. The women went back inside.

Sigrid was dead by the morning, and a coffin was made for her.

That same day some men went out fishing, and Thorstein of Lysufjord accompanied them down to the landing-place; and at dusk he went down again to see to the catch. Then Thorstein Eiriksson sent a message to him asking him to come back at once because there was trouble at home and Sigrid's corpse was trying to rise and get into bed with him. When he returned, she had reached the edge of Thorstein Eiriksson's bed; his namesake seized hold of her and drove an axe into her breast.

Thorstein Eiriksson died at nightfall. The other Thorstein told Gudrid to lie down and sleep, and said that he would keep vigil over the corpses during the night. She lay down, and fell asleep at once. Early that night the corpse of Thorstein Eiriksson sat up and spoke; he said that he wanted Gudrid to be summoned to him, for he wished to speak to her: 'God wills it that I be granted this hour to atone for my life.'

The other Thorstein went to Gudrid and roused her. He told her to cross herself and pray for God's help: 'Thorstein Eiriksson has told me that he wants to talk to you,' he said. 'You must decide for yourself; I cannot direct you one way or another.'

Gudrid replied, 'It is not unlikely that this strange occurrence will lead to something that will long be remembered afterwards. But I have faith that God will protect me. With God's mercy I shall take the risk of talking to him, for I shall not be able to escape harm if that is what is intended for me. Least of all do I want his corpse to walk abroad, which I suspect will happen otherwise.'[1]

Gudrid went in to see Thorstein. It seemed to her that he was shedding tears. He whispered in her ear a few words that she alone could hear, and then said that blessed were they who were true to their faith, for that way came help and mercy; but, he said, there were many who did not observe the faith properly:

'It is a bad custom, as has been done in Greenland since Christianity came here, to bury people in unconsecrated ground with scarcely any funeral rites. I want to be taken to church, along with the other people who have died here – all except Gardi, whom I want to have burned on a pyre as soon as possible, for he is responsible for all the hauntings that have gone on here this winter.'

He also told her about her future, and said that she would have a great destiny; but he warned her against marrying a Greenlander.

He also urged her to give their money to the church, or to the poor; and then he fell back for a second time.

It had been the custom in Greenland since Christianity came there to bury people in unconsecrated ground near the farms where they died; a stake was driven into the ground above the dead person's breast and later, when the priests arrived, the stake would be pulled out and holy water poured down the hole and funeral rites performed, however long after the burial it might then be.

The bodies were taken to the church at Eiriksfjord, and funeral rites were performed over them by priests.

Some time later Thorbjorn Vifilsson died, and Gudrid inherited everything. Eirik the Red received her at Brattahlid and looked after her affairs well.

1. *aptrganga*, 'return after death': in Icelandic folk-belief, it was the actual corpse of the dead person that could become active, not only his spirit. Cf. Gunnar of Hlidarend composing verses in his burial mound (*Njal's Saga*, Chapter 78), and the *locus classicus* – Grettir's fight with Glam (*Grettir's Saga*, Chapter 35).

7
Karlsefni in Greenland

A man called Thorfinn Karlsefni was the son of Thord Horse-Head who lived at Reyniness, north in Skagafjord, at a place now called [Stad]. Karlsefni was a very wealthy man, of noble lineage; his mother was called Thorunn.[1]

Karlsefni was a sea-going merchant and was considered a trader of great distinction. One summer he prepared his ship for a voyage to Greenland; Snorri Thorbrandsson of Alptafjord joined him, and they had forty men with them.

A man called Bjarni Grimolfsson, from Breidafjord, and his partner, a man called Thorhall Gamlason, from the Eastfjords, also made their ship ready for a voyage to Greenland that summer, with forty men on board.

When all was ready the two ships put out to sea. There is no report of how long they were at sea, but both ships reached Eiriksfjord in the autumn.

Eirik and some other settlers rode down to the ships and the trading went well. The captains invited Eirik to have whatever he wished from their cargoes; Eirik was not to be outdone in generosity and invited both crews to be his guests at Brattahlid for the winter. The traders accepted the invitation and went home with Eirik. Their goods were brought up to Brattahlid

---

1. The difference between S and H are most marked in the next three chapters; in H, the end of Chapter 7 and the whole of Chapters 8 and 9 were transcribed by Hauk Erlendsson himself (see pp. 30–1). H gives here a much fuller genealogy for Thorfinn Karlsefni, Hauk Erlendsson's ancestor.

There was a man called Thord, who lived at Hofdi, in Hofdastrand. He was married to Fridgerd, the daughter of Thorir Hima and of Fridgerd, the daughter of King Kjarval of Ireland. Thord was the son of Bjorn Butter-Box, the son of Thorvald Backbone, the son of Aslak, the son of Bjorn Iron-Side, the son of Ragnar Hairy-Breeks. Thord and Fridgerd had a son called Snorri, who married Thorhild Rjupa, the daughter of Thord Gellir; their son was Thord Horse-Head, who was the father of Thorfinn Karlsefni. Karlsefni's mother was called Thorunn.

where there were plenty of fine large outhouses to store them.[1]

The traders spent a pleasant winter there with Eirik. But as Christmas drew near, Eirik became much less cheerful than usual. One day Karlsefni spoke to Eirik and said, 'Is there something wrong, Eirik? I feel that you are in rather lower spirits than you have been. You have treated us with great hospitality and it is our duty to return your kindness as best we can. Tell me now, what is the cause of your worry?'

'You have accepted my hospitality with courtesy and good grace,' replied Eirik, 'and it does not occur to me to think that our dealings with one another will bring you any discredit. Rather, it is this: I should not like it to be said that you have had to endure such a meagre Christmas as the one that is now approaching.'[2]

'There is no question of that, Eirik,' said Karlsefni. 'We have malt and flour and grain in our cargoes and you are welcome to have as much of them as you wish and prepare as rich a feast as your generosity demands.'

Eirik accepted the offer and a Christmas feast was prepared. It was so lavish that people thought they had scarcely ever seen one so magnificent before.[3]

After Christmas Karlsefni approached Eirik and asked for the hand of Gudrid Thorbjorn's-daughter, whom he regarded as being under Eirik's care, for he thought the woman good-looking and capable. Eirik replied that he would fully support the proposal and said that she was worthy of a good match: 'And it is likely that she is fulfilling her destiny if she marries you,' he said. He also said that he had heard good reports of Karlsefni.

The proposal was put to her and she agreed to accept Eirik's advice; and not to make a long story of it the outcome was that the marriage took place, and the Christmas feast was extended into a wedding feast.

They all had a splendid time at Brattahlid that winter; there

1. Archaeologists have unearthed the remains of four large barns at the site of Eirik's farm at Brattahlid.

2. H adds: *when Eirik the Red was your host at Brattahlid in Greenland.*

3. H adds: *in a poor country.*

was much chess-playing and story-telling, and many other entertainments that enrich a household.[1]

8

Karlsefni goes to Vinland

There were great discussions at Brattahlid that winter about going in search of Vinland[2] where, it was said, there was excellent land to be had. The outcome was that Karlsefni and Snorri Thorbrandsson prepared their ship and made ready to search for Vinland that summer.[3]

Bjarni Grimolfsson and Thorhall Gamlason[4] decided to join the expedition with their own ship and the crew they had brought from Iceland.

There was a man named Thorvard, who was Eirik the Red's son-in-law.[5]

There was another man named Thorhall, who was known as Thorhall the Hunter; he had been in Eirik's service for a long time, acting as his huntsman in summer, and had many responsibilities. He was a huge man, swarthy and uncouth; he was getting old now, bad-tempered and cunning, taciturn as a rule but abusive when he spoke, and always a trouble-maker. He had not had much to do with Christianity since it had come to Greenland. He was not particularly popular, but Eirik and he had always been close friends. He went with Thorvald and

1. Chessmen carved from walrus ivory and whalebone have been unearthed at sites in Greenland. Others from the Viking period have been found in Scandinavia and the Hebrides (some of which are to be seen in the British Museum, and the National Museum of Antiquities for Scotland, in Edinburgh).

2. H – *Vinland the Good*. This is the first mention of the name Vinland in *Eirik's Saga*.

3. Snorri Thorbrandsson's journey to Greenland and Vinland is mentioned in *Eyrbyggja Saga*, Chapter 48.

4. In *Grettir's Saga*, a man called Thorhall Gamlason, who plays a minor part in it, is known as 'the Vinlander'.

5. H reads: *who was married to Freydis, an illegitimate daughter of Eirik the Red. Thorvard also joined them, as did Thorvald, a son of Eirik the Red.*

the others because he had considerable experience of wild regions.[1]

They had the ship that Thorbjorn Vifilsson had brought from Iceland, and when they joined Karlsefni there were mostly Greenlanders on board. Altogether there were 160 people taking part in this expedition.

They sailed first up to the Western Settlement, and then to the Bjarn Isles.[2] From there they sailed before a northerly wind and after two days at sea they sighted land and rowed ashore in boats to explore it. They found there many slabs of stone so huge that two men could stretch out on them sole to sole.[3] There were numerous foxes there. They gave this country a name and called it *Helluland*.

From there they sailed for two days before a northerly wind[4] and sighted land ahead; this was a heavily-wooded country abounding with animals. There was an island to the south-east, where they found bears, and so they named it *Bjarn Isle*; they named the wooded mainland itself *Markland*.

After two days they sighted land again and held in towards it; it was a promontory they were approaching. They tacked along the coast, with the land to starboard.[5]

It was open and harbourless, with long beaches and extensive sands. They went ashore in boats and found a ship's keel on the headland, and so they called the place *Kjalarness*. They called this stretch of coast *Furdustrands*[6] because it took so long to

1. The Norsemen in Greenland explored the area very extensively: cf. the fourteenth-century runic inscription in Baffin Bay, on the Arctic island of Kingiktorssoak (see p. 21).

2. H reads: *Bjarn Isle*. This could be Disco Island, off the west coast of Greenland, or any cluster of islets off the east coast of Baffin Island. It has so far proved impossible to identify any of the Norse landfalls beyond dispute; see List of Proper Names.

3. H reads: *huge slabs of stone, many of them twelve ells across* (i.e. eighteen feet).

4. H reads: *From there they sailed for two days, first south and then shifting course to south-east.*

5. H reads: *From there they sailed south along the coast for a long time until they came to a promontory; the mainland lay to starboard.*

6. Literally, 'Marvel Strands'. See List of Proper Names.

sail past it. Then the coastline became indented with bays and they steered into one of them.

When Leif Eirikson had been with King Olaf Tryggvason and had been asked to preach Christianity in Greenland, the king had given him a Scottish couple, a man called Haki and a woman called Hekja. The king told Leif to use them if he ever needed speed, for they could run faster than deer. Leif and Eirik had turned them over to Karlsefni for this expedition.

When the ships had passed Furdustrands the two Scots were put ashore and told to run southwards to explore the country's resources, and to return within three days. They each wore a garment called a *bjafal*,[1] which had a hood at the top and was open at the sides; it had no sleeves and was fastened between the legs with a loop and button. That was all they wore.

The ships cast anchor there and waited, and after three days the Scots came running down to the shore; one of them was carrying some grapes, and the other some wild wheat. They told Karlsefni that they thought they had found good land.

They were taken on board, and the expedition sailed on until they reached a fjord. They steered their ships into it. At its mouth lay an island around which there flowed very strong currents, and so they named it *Straum Island*. There were so many birds[2] on it that one could scarcely set foot between their eggs.

They steered into the fjord, which they named *Straumfjord*; here they unloaded their ships and settled down. They had brought with them livestock of all kinds and they looked around for natural produce. There were mountains there and the country was beautiful to look at, and they paid no attention to anything except exploring it. There was tall grass everywhere.

They stayed there that winter, which turned out to be a very severe one; they had made no provision for it during the summer, and now they ran short of food and the hunting failed. They moved out to the island in the hope of finding game, or

1. H – *kjafal*, which has been compared with Irish *cabhail*, meaning 'trunk of a shirt', or Irish *giobhail*, 'garment'.
2. H – *eiderduck*.

stranded whales, but there was little food to be found there, although their livestock throve. Then they prayed to God to send them something to eat, but the response was not as prompt as they would have liked.

Meanwhile Thorhall the Hunter disappeared and they went out to search for him. They searched for three days; and on the fourth day Karlsefni and Bjarni found him on top of a cliff. He was staring up at the sky with eyes and mouth and nostrils agape, scratching himself and pinching himself and mumbling. They asked him what he was doing there; he replied that it was no concern of theirs, and told them not to be surprised and that he was old enough not to need them to look after him. They urged him to come back home with them, and he did.

A little later a whale was washed up and they rushed to cut it up. No one recognized what kind of a whale it was, not even Karlsefni, who was an expert on whales. The cooks boiled the meat, but when it was eaten it made them all ill.

Then Thorhall the Hunter walked over and said, 'Has not Redbeard[1] turned out to be more successful than your Christ? This was my reward for the poem I composed in honour of my patron, Thor; he has seldom failed me.'

When the others realized this they refused to use the whale-meat and threw it over a cliff, and committed themselves to God's mercy. Then a break came in the weather to allow them to go out fishing, and after that there was no scarcity of provisions.

In the spring they went back to Straumfjord and gathered supplies, game on the mainland, eggs on the island, and fish from the sea.

9
Thorhall breaks away

They now discussed where to go, and laid their plans. Thorhall the Hunter wanted to go north beyond Furdustrands and Kjalarness to search for Vinland there, but Karlsefni wanted to

1. A familiar name for the god Thor.

follow the coast farther south, for he believed that the country would improve the farther south they went, and thought it advisable to explore both possibilities.

Thorhall prepared his ship in the lee of the island; there were only nine others who joined him – the rest all went with Karlsefni.

One day, as Thorhall was carrying water on board, he drank some of it and then said :

> 'These oak-hearted warriors
> Lured me to this land
> With promise of choice drinks;
> Now I could curse this country!
> For I, the helmet-wearer,
> Must now grovel at a spring
> And wield a water-pail;
> No wine has touched my lips.'

Then they put to sea, and Karlsefni accompanied them as far as the island. Before they hoisted sail, Thorhall said :

> 'Let us head back
> To our countrymen at home;
> Let our ocean-striding ship
> Explore the broad tracts of the sea
> While these eager swordsmen
> Who laud these lands
> Settle in Furdustrands
> And boil up whales.'

With that they parted company. Thorhall and his crew sailed northward past Furdustrands and Kjalarness, and tried to beat westward from there.[1] But they ran into fierce head-winds and were driven right across to Ireland. There they were brutally beaten and enslaved; and there Thorhall died.

10

Karlsefni goes south

Karlsefni sailed south along the coast, accompanied by Snorri and Bjarni and the rest of the expedition. They sailed for a long

1. It looks as if Thorhall thought that Vinland lay somewhere in the Gulf of St Lawrence.

time and eventually came to a river that flowed down into a lake and from the lake into the sea. There were extensive sand-bars outside the river mouth, and ships could only enter it at high tide.

Karlsefni and his men sailed into the estuary and named the place *Hope* (Tidal Lake). Here they found wild wheat growing in fields on all the low ground and grape vines on all the higher ground. Every stream was teeming with fish. They dug trenches at the high-tide mark, and when the tide went out there were halibut trapped in the trenches. In the woods there was a great number of animals of all kinds.

They stayed there for a fortnight, enjoying themselves and noticing nothing untoward. They had their livestock with them. But early one morning as they looked around they caught sight of nine[1] skin-boats; the men in them were waving sticks which made a noise like flails, and the motion was sunwise.[2]

Karlsefni said, 'What can this signify?'

'It could well be a token of peace,' said Snorri. 'Let us take a white shield and go to meet them with it.'

They did so. The newcomers rowed towards them and stared at them in amazement as they came ashore. They were small[3] and evil-looking, and their hair was coarse; they had large eyes and broad cheekbones. They stayed there for a while, marvelling, and then rowed away south round the headland.

Karlsefni and his men had built their settlement on a slope by the lakeside; some of the houses were close to the lake, and others were farther away. They stayed there that winter. There was no snow at all, and all the livestock were able to fend for themselves.

1. H – *a great number of.*
2. Native Americans are known to have used rattle-sticks during various rituals, which may well be the explanation of this threshing sound the Norsemen could hear.
3. H – *dark-coloured.*

The Skrælings attack

Then, early one morning in spring, they saw a great horde of skin-boats approaching from the south round the headland, so dense that it looked as if the estuary were strewn with charcoal; and sticks were being waved from every boat. Karlsefni's men raised their shields and the two parties began to trade.

What the natives wanted most to buy was red cloth; they also wanted to buy swords and spears, but Karlsefni and Snorri forbade that. In exchange for the cloth they traded grey pelts. The natives took a span[1] of red cloth for each pelt, and tied the cloth round their heads. The trading went on like this for a while until the cloth began to run short; then Karlsefni and his men cut it up into pieces which were no more than a finger's breadth wide; but the Skrælings paid just as much or even more for it.

Then it so happened that a bull belonging to Karlsefni and his men came running out of the woods, bellowing furiously. The Skrælings were terrified and ran to their skin-boats and rowed away south round the headland.

After that there was no sign of the natives for three whole weeks. But then Karlsefni's men saw a huge number of boats coming from the south, pouring in like a torrent. This time all the sticks were being waved anti-clockwise and all the Skrælings were howling loudly. Karlsefni and his men now hoisted red shields and advanced towards them.

When they clashed there was a fierce battle and a hail of missiles came flying over, for the Skrælings were using catapults. Karlsefni and Snorri saw them hoist a large sphere on a pole;[2] it was dark blue in colour. It came flying in over the heads of Karlsefni's men and made an ugly din when it struck the ground.[3] This terrified Karlsefni and his men so much that

1. About nine inches.
2. H adds: *it was the size of a sheep's stomach.*
3. This device has been compared with the ballista which ancient traditions of the Algonquin tribe describe.

their only thought was to flee, and they retreated farther up the river.[1] They did not halt until they reached some cliffs, where they prepared to make a resolute stand.

Freydis came out and saw the retreat. She shouted, 'Why do you flee from such pitiful wretches, brave men like you? You should be able to slaughter them like cattle. If I had weapons, I am sure I could fight better than any of you.'

The men paid no attention to what she was saying. Freydis tried to join them but she could not keep up with them because she was pregnant. She was following them into the woods when the Skrælings closed in on her. In front of her lay a dead man, Thorbrand Snorrason, with a flintstone buried in his head, and his sword beside him. She snatched up the sword and prepared to defend herself. When the Skrælings came rushing towards her she pulled one of her breasts out of her bodice and slapped it with the sword. The Skrælings were terrified at the sight of this and fled back to their boats and hastened away.

Karlsefni and his men came over to her and praised her courage. Two of their men had been killed, and four[2] of the Skrælings, even though Karlsefni and his men had been fighting against heavy odds.

They returned to their houses and pondered what force it was that had attacked them from inland; they then realized that the only attackers had been those who had come in the boats, and that the other force had just been a delusion.

The Skrælings found the other dead Norseman, with his axe lying beside him.[3] One of them hacked at a rock with the axe, and the axe broke; and thinking it worthless now because it could not withstand stone, they threw it away.

Karlsefni and his men had realized by now that although the land was excellent they could never live there in safety or freedom from fear, because of the native inhabitants. So they made ready to leave the place and return home. They sailed off

1. H adds: *for they were sure that the Skrælings were attacking them from all sides.*

2. H – *a great many.*

3. H adds: *one of them picked it up and chopped at a tree with it, and then each one of them in turn tried it; they all thought it a wonderful find, because of its sharpness.*

north along the coast. They came upon five Skrælings clad in skins, asleep; beside them were containers full of deer-marrow mixed with blood.[1] Karlsefni's men reckoned that these five must be outlaws, and killed them.

Then they came to a headland on which there were numerous deer; the headland looked like a huge cake of dung, for the animals used to spend the winters there.

Soon afterwards Karlsefni and his men arrived at Straumfjord, where they found plenty of everything.

According to some people, Bjarni Grimolfsson and Freydis[2] had stayed behind there with a hundred people and gone no farther while Karlsefni and Snorri had sailed south with forty men and, after spending barely two months at Hope, had returned that same summer.

Karlsefni set out with one ship in search of Thorhall the Hunter, while the rest of the company stayed behind. He sailed north past Kjalarness and then bore west, with the land on the port beam. It was a region of wild and desolate woodland; and when they had travelled a long way they came to a river which flowed from east to west into the sea. They steered into the river mouth and lay to by its southern bank.

12

Thorvald Eiriksson dies

One morning Karlsefni and his men saw something glittering on the far side of the clearing, and they shouted at it. It moved, and it proved to be a Uniped;[3] it came bounding down towards

1. This food has been identified with the Native American food *pemmican* – cakes of dried meat mixed with marrow-grease, which they used as iron rations on hunting expeditions.

2. H – *Gudrid*.

3. This incongruous reference to Unipeds is symptomatic of the author's fondness for medieval learning (see p. 39). It is interesting to note that Unipeds figure in an Icelandic translation of a medieval geographical treatise (ultimately based on the works of the seventh-century scholar Isidore of Seville); the Icelandic version, which is considerably older than *Eirik's Saga*, is contained in *Hauksbók*. Unipeds were said to live in Africa (see p. 39).

where the ship lay. Thorvald, Eirik the Red's son, was sitting at the helm. The Uniped shot an arrow into his groin.

Thorvald pulled out the arrow and said, 'This is a rich country we have found; there is plenty of fat around my entrails.' Soon afterwards he died of the wound.

The Uniped ran off to the north. Karlsefni and his men gave chase, catching occasional glimpses of it as it fled. Then it disappeared into a creek and the pursuers turned back. One of the men uttered this stanza:

> 'Yes, it's true
> That our men chased
> A Uniped
> Down to the sea;
> The weird creature
> Ran like the wind
> Over rough ground;
> Hear that, Karlsefni.'

Then they sailed away north and thought they could see Uniped-Land; but they decided not to risk the lives of the crew any further. They reckoned that the mountains they could see there roughly corresponded with those at Hope and were part of the same range, and they estimated that both regions were equidistant from Straumfjord.

They returned to Straumfjord and spent the third winter there. But now quarrels broke out frequently; those who were unmarried kept pestering the married men.

It was in the first autumn that Karlsefni's son, Snorri, was born; he was three years old when they left.

They set sail before a southerly wind and reached Markland, where they came upon five Skrælings – a bearded man, two women, and two children. Karlsefni and his men captured the two boys, but the others got away and sank down into the ground.

They took the boys with them and taught them the language, and baptized them. The boys said that their mother was called Vætild and their father Ovægir. They said that the land of the Skrælings was ruled by two kings, one of whom was called Avaldamon and the other Valdidida. They said that there were no houses there and that people lived in caves or holes in the ground. They said that there was a country across from their own land where the people went about in white clothing and uttered loud cries and carried poles with patches of cloth attached. This is thought to have been *Hvítramannaland*.[1]

Finally they reached Greenland, and spent the winter with Eirik the Red.

13

Bjarni Grimolfsson's death

Bjarni Grimolfsson's ship was blown into the Greenland Sea.[2] They found themselves in waters infested with maggots, and before they knew it the ship was riddled under them and had begun to sink.

They discussed what they should do. They had one ship's-boat which had been treated with tar made from seal-blubber; it is said that shell-maggots cannot penetrate timber which has been so treated. Most of the crew said that they should fill this boat with as many people as it would hold; but when this was tried they found that the boat would not hold more than half of them.

Then Bjarni said that the people who were to go should be chosen by lot, and not by rank.

But everyone tried to get into the boat. The boat, however, would not hold them all and so they agreed to this suggestion of drawing lots for places in it. When the lots were drawn it

1. Literally, 'White Men's Land'. H adds : *or Greater Ireland*. The concept of a country of White men (Albania-land) occurs in Icelandic versions of medieval European works of learning and was associated with Asia, somewhere to the north of India. In *Landnámabók*, however, there is a reference to a *Hvítramannaland* which was said to lie six days' sail west of Ireland. There may well be a connexion between this reference and the *Tír na bhFear bhFionn* (Land of the White Men) of Irish Legend, particularly in view of *Hauksbók*'s alternative designation for it of 'Greater Ireland'.

2. H – *the sea west of Ireland*. This chapter was considerably condensed and re-written by Hauk Erlendsson in H.

so happened that Bjarni himself, along with nearly half the crew, drew a place, and these all left the ship for the boat. When they were in the boat one young Icelander who had been Bjarni's companion said, 'Are you going to leave me here, Bjarni?'

'That is how it has to be,' replied Bjarni.

The Icelander said, 'But that is not what you promised when I left my father's farm in Iceland to go with you.'

'I see no other way,' said Bjarni. 'What do you suggest?'

'I suggest we change places; you come up here and I shall go down there.'

'So be it,' said Bjarni. 'I can see that you would spare no effort to live, and are afraid to die.'

So they changed places. The Icelander stepped into the boat and Bjarni went back on board the ship; and it is said that Bjarni and all those who were on the ship with him perished there in the maggot sea.

Those in the ship's-boat sailed away and reached land,[1] where they recounted this story.

14

Karlsefni's descendants

The second summer after this, Karlsefni went back to Iceland with his son Snorri and went to his farm at Reyniness. Karlsefni's mother felt he had married beneath him, and she stayed away from his home for the first winter. But when she realized what an exceptional woman Gudrid was she returned home, and they got on well together.

Snorri Karlsefnisson had a daughter called Hallfrid, who was the mother of Bishop Thorlak Runolfsson.

Karlsefni and Gudrid had another son, called Thorbjorn, who was the father of Thorunn, the mother of Bishop Bjorn.

Snorri Karlsefnisson had a son called Thorgeir, the father of Yngvild, the mother of the first Bishop Brand.[2]

1. H – *Dublin, in Ireland.*
2. Cf. *Grænlendinga Saga*, Chapter 9, where the genealogy was

And there this saga ends.[1]

clearly written before there was any question of a *second* Bishop Brand (Brand Jonsson, great-grandson of the first Bishop Brand, and bishop of Holar 1263–4).

1 H reads: *Snorri Karlsefnisson had another daughter, called Steinunn, who married Einar, the son of Grundar-Ketil, the son of Thorvald Hook, the son of Thorir of Espihill. Their son was Thorstein the Unjust; he was the father of Gudrun, who married Jorund of Keldur. Their daughter was Halla, the mother of Flosi, the father of Valgerd, the mother of Sir Erlend the Strong, the father of Hauk the Lawman. Another of Flosi's daughters was Thordis, the mother of Lady Ingigerd the Powerful; her daughter was Lady Hallbera, abbess at Stad, in Reyniness. Many other great people in Iceland are descended from Karlsefni and Gudrid, but not recorded here. May God be with us. Amen.*

LIST OF PROPER NAMES

This list is intended not as a complete index, but a quick guide to readers who may find the Icelandic names confusing at first. Each entry in the Personal Names section is in the form of a brief summary of the part played by that person in either or both of the sagas, and is listed under the Christian name. Those individuals mentioned only in the genealogies in the footnotes to the texts are not listed.

The entries in the Place Names section are confined to those places in Greenland and North America mentioned in the texts, and modern equivalents are suggested for them wherever possible; it should be remembered, however, that all the North American identifications are only tentative.

Grl refers to *Grœnlendinga Saga*, and *Eir* refers to *Eirik's Saga*; the numbers refer to chapters, not pages.

PERSONAL NAMES

ARNLAUG, one of the original settlers of Greenland, at Arnlaugsfjord, *Grl*, 1.

ARNORA, daughter of Einar of Laugarbrekka; marries Thorgeir Vifilsson, *Eir*, 3.

ASLAK OF LANGADALE, supports Thorgest against Eirik, *Eir*, 2.

ASVALD ULFSSON, grandfather of Erik, *Grl*, 1, *Eir*, 2.

AUD THE DEEP-MINDED, daughter of Ketil Flat-Nose; one of the original settlers of Iceland, gives land to Vifil, *Eir*, 1.

AVALDAMON, a Skræling king, *Eir*, 12.

BJARNI GRIMOLFSSON, from Breidafjord in Iceland; goes with his partner Thorhall Gamlason to Greenland, stays with Eirik, *Eir*, 7; joins Karlsefni's expedition to Vinland, *Eir*, 8; at Hope in Vinland, *Eir*, 10, or stayed behind at Straumfjord, *Eir*, 11; blown off course into the Greenland Sea, renounces his chance of safety, dies with half his crew, *Eir*, 13.

BJARNI HERJOLFSSON, an Icelandic merchant, son of Herjolf Bardarson, *Grl*, 2; sails from Iceland to join his father in Greenland, is driven off course, sights unknown lands, fails to explore them, reaches Greenland, settles at Herjolfsness, *Grl*, 2; goes to Earl Eirik's court in Norway, tells of his journey, returns to Greenland, *Grl*, 3; sells his ship to Leif Eiriksson for a Vinland expedition, *Grl*, 3.

BJORN (THE EASTERNER), son of Ketil Flat-Nose, brother of Aud the Deep-Minded; one of the original settlers in Iceland, *Eir*, 1.

BJORN GILSSON, bishop of Holar 1147–62; descendant of Karlsefni, *Grl*, 9, *Eir*, 14.

BJORN KARLSEFNISSON, son of Thorfinn Karlsefni, *Grl*, 9 (called Thorbjorn, *Eir*, 14).

BRAND SÆMUNDARSON, bishop of Holar 1163–1201; descendant of Karlsefni, *Grl*, 9, *Eir*, 14.

EINAR, one of the original settlers in Greenland, at Einarsfjord, *Grl*, 1.

EINAR OF LAUGARBREKKA, father-in-law of Thorbjorn and Thorgeir Vifilsson, *Eir*, 3.

EINAR THORGEIRSSON, of Thorgeirsfell, an Icelandic merchant; seeks the hand of Gudrid, is rejected, *Eir*, 3.

EIRIK (HAKONARSON), earl of Norway 1000–14; admits Bjarni Herjolfsson to his court, *Grl*, 3.

EIRIK THE RED, son of Thorvald Asvaldsson; leaves Norway with his father, settles at Drangar in Iceland, marries Thjodhild and moves south to Haukadale, is involved in killings and is banished, discovers Greenland and colonizes it, settles at Brattahlid in Eiriksfjord, *Grl*, 1, *Eir* 2; has a son called Leif, *Grl*, 1; Eirik's children listed – Leif, Thorvald, Thorstein, Freydis, *Grl*, 2, Thorstein, Leif, *Eir*, 5 (Thorvald and Freydis added, *Eir*, 8, 11, 12); resents Christianity, *Eir*, 5; agrees to join Leif on an expedition to Vinland but changes his mind, *Grl*, 3 (sets out for Vinland with his son Thorstein but returns in the autumn, *Eir*, 5); gives his daughter-in-law Gudrid a home at Brattahlid, *Eir*, 6; entertains Karlsefni and two Icelandic crews, gives a Christmas feast, marries Gudrid to Karlsefni, *Eir*, 7; entertains Karlsefni and the Vinland colonizers on their return from Vinland, *Eir*, 12; dies, *Grl*, 4; is said to have died before Greenland became Christian, *Grl*, 5.

EYJOLF OF SVIN ISLAND, supports Eirik against Thorgest, *Grl*, 1, *Eir*, 2; hides Eirik from his enemies, *Eir*, 2.

EYJOLF SAUR, kinsman of Valthjof of Valthjofstead, kills Eirik's slaves, is killed by Eirik, *Grl*, 1, *Eir*, 2.

EYVIND THE EASTERNER, father-in-law of Thorstein the Red, *Eir*, 1.

FINNBOGI, an Icelandic merchant; sails with his brother Helgi to Greenland, joins Freydis' expedition to Vinland, is murdered there at her instigation, *Grl*, 8.

FREYDIS, daughter of Eirik the Red (illegitimate, *Eir*, 8), married to Thorvard of Gardar, *Grl*, 2, *Eir*, 8; joins Thorvard on Karlsefni's expedition to Vinland, *Eir*, 8; defies Skrælings when pregnant, *Eir*, 11; makes a separate expedition to Vinland with Finnbogi and Helgi, murders them, returns to Greenland, *Grl*, 8; her atrocities exposed, *Grl*, 9.

FRIDREK, a German bishop, first Christian missionary to Iceland; forced to flee the country, *Grl*, 1.

GARDI, overseer at Lysufjord; dies of disease, haunts the farm, *Eir*, 6.

GEIRSTEIN OF JORVI, kinsman of Eyjolf Saur; outlaws Eirik from Haukadale, *Eir*, 2.

GRIMHILD, wife of Thorstein of Lysufjord; dies of disease, *Grl*, 6. (Called Sigrid in *Eir*, 6.)

GROA, daughter of Thorstein the Red; marries in Orkney, *Eir*, 1.

GUDRID, daughter of Thorbjorn Vifilsson; fostered by Orm of Arnarstapi, wooed by Einar Thorgeirsson, his suit rejected, goes with her parents to Greenland, *Eir*, 3; assists sybil at Herjolfsness, hears her future prophesied, *Eir*, 4; is said to be wife of Thorir the Norwegian and rescued from shipwreck by Leif Eiriksson, is widowed, *Grl*, 4; marries Thorstein Eiriksson, *Grl*, 6, *Eir*, 6; accompanies Thorstein on unsuccessful journey to Vinland, *Grl*, 6; goes to Lysufjord in Western Settlement where Thorstein dies and prophesies her future, returns to Brattahlid, *Grl*, 6, *Eir*, 6; marries Thorfinn Karlsefni,

Grl, 7, *Eir*, 7; accompanies Karlsefni to Vinland, *Grl*, 7, *Eir*, 12; gives birth to son Snorri in Vinland, *Grl*, 7, *Eir*, 12; sees apparition of woman, *Grl*, 7; returns with Karlsefni to Iceland, their descendants listed, *Grl*, 9, *Eir*, 14; goes on pilgrimage to Rome, becomes an anchoress, *Grl*, 9; wins over her mother-in-law, *Eir*, 14.

GUDRID, woman who appears in apparition to Gudrid Thorbjorn's-daughter in Vinland, *Grl*, 7.

GUNNBJORN ULFSSON, discoverer of the Gunnbjarnar Skerries off Greenland, *Grl*, 1, *Eir*, 2.

HAFGRIM, one of the original settlers of Greenland, at Hafgrimsfjord and Vatna District, *Grl*, 1.

HAKI, Scottish slave owned by Leif Eiriksson; sent by Karlsefni to reconnoitre Vinland, *Eir*, 8.

HALLDIS, wife of Orm of Arnarstapi; Gudrid's foster-mother, emigrates to Greenland, dies at sea, *Eir*, 3; taught Gudrid the Warlock-songs, *Eir*, 4.

HALLFRID, daughter of Snorri Karlsefnisson and mother of Bishop Thorlak, *Grl*, 9, *Eir*, 14.

HALLVEIG, daughter of Einar of Laugarbrekka; marries Thorbjorn Vifilsson, mother of Gudrid, *Eir*, 3.

HEKJA, a Scottish bondwoman; sent by Karlsefni to reconnoitre Vinland, *Eir*, 8.

HELGI, an Icelandic merchant; sails with brother Finnbogi to Greenland, joins Freydis' expedition to Vinland, is murdered there at her instigation, *Grl*, 8.

HELGI THORBRANDSSON, son of Thorbrand of Alptafjord; one of the original settlers of Greenland, at Alptafjord, *Grl*, 1; supports Eirik against Thorgest, *Grl*, 1, *Eir*, 2.

HERJOLF BARDARSON, father of Bjarni Herjolfsson; one of the original settlers of Greenland, at Herjolfsness, *Grl*, 1, 2.

HRAFN THE DUELLER, killed by Eirik, *Grl*, 1, *Eir*, 2.

HRAFN, one of the original settlers of Greenland, at Hrafnsfjord, *Grl*, 1.

ILLUGI, son of Aslak of Langadale; supports Thorgest against Eirik, *Eir*, 2.

INGJALD HELGASON, a king, father of Olaf the White, *Eir*, 1.

INGOLF OF HOLMLATUR, shelters Eirik on his return from outlawry, *Eir*, 2.

KARLSEFNI, *see* Thorfinn Karlsefni.

KETIL, one of the original settlers of Greenland, at Ketilsfjord, *Grl*, 1.

KETIL FLAT-NOSE, father of Aud the Deep-Minded, *Eir*, 1.

LEIF EIRIKSSON (Leif the Lucky), son of Eirik the Red, *Grl*, 1, 2, *Eir*, 5; explores lands sighted by Bjarni Herjolfsson, names Helluland, Markland, and Vinland, builds Leif's Houses, rescues Thorir and Gudrid off mid-ocean reef, earns nickname Leif the Lucky, *Grl*, 3–4; sails from Greenland to Norway, begets son in the Hebrides, is converted by King Olaf Tryggvason, returns to Greenland to evangelize but discovers unknown lands on the way, takes samples of grapes, wild wheat, and maples, rescues shipwrecked sailors, converts Greenland to Christianity, earns nickname Leif the Lucky, *Eir*, 5; lends Thorvald his ship to go to Vinland, *Grl*, 4; lends Thorstein his ship for a Vinland voyage, *Grl*, 6; marries Gudrid to Karlsefni, *Grl*, 7; allows Thorvald, Karlsefni, and Freydis to use Leif's Houses, *Grl*, 5, 7, 8; exposes Freydis' crimes in Vinland, *Grl*, 9.

ODD OF JORVI, kinsman of Eyjolf Saur; outlaws Eirik from Haukadale, *Eir*, 2.

OLAF THE WHITE, Norse warrior king, husband of Aud the Deep-Minded; captures Dublin, killed in battle in Ireland, *Eir*, 1.

OLAF TRYGGVASON, king of Norway 995–1000; host to Leif Eiriksson, sends him to Greenland to preach Christianity, *Eir*, 5; gives Leif a Scottish couple as slaves, *Eir*, 8.

ORM OF ARNARSTAPI, an Iceland farmer; foster-father to Gudrid, supports marriage-offer from Einar Thorgeirsson, is snubbed by Gudrid's father; emigrates to Greenland with Thorbjorn Vifilsson, dies at sea, *Eir*, 3.

OVÆGIR, father of the captured Skræling children, *Eir*, 12.

RUNOLF THORLEIKSSON, father of Bishop Thorlak, *Grl*, 9, *Eir*, 14.

SIGRID, wife of Thorstein of Lysufjord; dies of disease, *Eir*, 6. (Called Grimhild in *Grl*, 6.)

SIGURD THE POWERFUL, earl of Orkney (d. 875); allied with Thorstein the Red, *Eir*, 1.

SNORRI KARLSEFNISSON, son of Thorfinn Karlsefni; born in Vinland, *Grl*, 7, *Eir*, 12; three years old when he leaves Vinland, *Eir*, 12; takes over his father's farm in Iceland, *Grl*, 9; his descendants, *Grl*, 9, *Eir*, 14.

SNORRI THORBRANDSSON, son of Thorbrand of Alptafjord; supports Eirik against Thorgest, *Grl*, 1, *Eir*, 2; accompanies Karlsefni to Greenland, *Eir*, 7; joins Karlsefni's expedition to Vinland, *Eir*, 8; fights the Skrælings, his son Thorbrand killed by them, *Eir*, 10–11.

SOLVI, one of the original settlers of Greenland, at Solvadale, *Grl*, 1.

STYR THORGRIMSSON, supports Eirik against Thorgest, *Grl*, 1, *Eir*, 2.

THJODHILD, wife of Eirik the Red, *Grl*, 1, *Eir*, 2, 5; embraces Christianity, refuses to live with Eirik, builds Thjodhild's Church near Brattahlid, *Eir*, 5.

THORBJORG (the Little Sybil), prophetess in Greenland; attends a feast at Herjolfsness, prophesies Gudrid's future, *Eir*, 4.

THORBJORN GLORA, one of the original settlers of Greenland, at Siglufjord, *Grl*, 1.

THORBJORN KARLSEFNISSON, son of Thorfinn Karlsefni, *Eir*, 14. (Called Bjorn, *Grl*, 9.)

THORBJORN VIFILSSON, son of Vifil of Vifilsdale, *Eir*, 1; supports Eirik against Thorgest, *Grl*, 1, *Eir*, 2; marries Hallveig, moves to Hellisvellir in Laugarbrekka, *Eir*, 3; father of Gudrid, *Eir*, 3, *Grl*, 6; rejects Einar Thorgeirsson as Gudrid's suitor, emigrates to Greenland, lands at Herjolfsness, *Eir*, 3; refuses to witness Thorbjorg's sorcery, sails to Eiriksfjord, settles at Stokkaness, *Eir*, 4; his ship used by Thorstein Eiriksson for Vinland voyage, *Eir*, 5; dies, *Eir*, 6; his ship used in Karlsefni's expedition to Vinland, *Eir*, 8.

THORBRAND OF ALPTAFJORD; his sons support Eirik against Thorgest, *Grl*, 1, *Eir*, 2; his son Helgi settles in Greenland, *Grl*, 1; his son Snorri accompanies Karlsefni to Greenland and Vinland, *Eir*, 7, 8.

THORBRAND SNORRASON, son of Snorri Thorbrandsson; killed by Skrælings in Vinland, *Eir*, 11.

THORD GELLIR, his sons support Thorgest against Eirik, *Grl*, 1, *Eir*, 2; great-grandfather of Karlsefni, *Eir*, 7 (footnote).

THORD HORSE-HEAD, father of Thorfinn Karlsefni, *Grl*, 7, *Eir*, 7.

THORFINN KARLSEFNI, an Icelandic merchant; arrives in Greenland, is entertained at Brattahlid by Leif Eiriksson, *Grl*, 7 (by Eirik the Red, *Eir*, 7); marries Gudrid, *Grl*, 7, *Eir*, 7; leads an expedition of one ship to Vinland, trades with Skrælings, fights with them, returns to Greenland, *Grl*, 7; leads an expedition of three ships to Vinland, calling at Western Settlement, Helluland, and Markland, stays at Straumfjord and Hope, trades with Skrælings, fights with them, searches for Thorhall the Hunter, sees a Uniped and sights Uniped-Land, returns to Markland, captures two Skræling children, reaches Greenland, *Eir*, 8–12; goes to Norway, *Grl*, 8; sells his gable-head there, *Grl*, 9; comes to Iceland and settles there, his descendants listed, *Grl*, 9, *Eir*, 14.

THORGEIR OF HITARDALE, supports Thorgest against Eirik, *Grl*, 1, *Eir*, 2.

THORGEIR OF THORGEIRSFELL, a freed slave; father of Einar Thorgeirsson, *Eir*, 3.

THORGEIR SNORRASON, son of Snorri Karlsefnisson, *Grl*, 9, *Eir*, 14.

THORGEIR VIFILSSON, son of Vifil of Vifilsdale, *Eir*, 1; marries Arnora, daughter of Einar of Laugarbrekka, *Eir*, 3.

THORGERD, wife of Herjolf Bardarson, mother of Bjarni Herjolfsson, *Grl*, 2.

THORGEST OF BREIDABOLSTEAD; borrows Eirik's bench-boards, refuses to return them, fights pitched battle with Eirik, *Grl*, 1, *Eir*, 2; loses two sons in that battle, hounds Eirik from Iceland, *Eir*, 2; fights Eirik again when Eirik returns from exile, defeats him, is reconciled with him, *Eir*, 2.

THORGILS LEIFSSON, illegitmate son of Leif Eiriksson and Thorgunna; goes to Iceland and Greenland, *Eir*, 5.

THORGUNNA, a Hebridean woman; has a son, Thorgils, by Leif, *Eir*, 5.

THORHALL GAMLASON, an Icelandic merchant; goes to Greenland with Bjarni Grimolfsson, *Eir*, 7; joins Karlsefni's expedition to Vinland, *Eir*, 8.

THORHALL THE HUNTER, a member of Eirik's household; takes part in Karlsefni's expedition to Vinland, *Eir*, 8; separates, sails north to Furdustrands, is blown off course to Ireland, is beaten to death there, *Eir*, 9.

THORIR THE EASTERNER, a Norwegian merchant; husband of Gudrid, is rescued from shipwreck by Leif Eiriksson, dies, *Grl*, 4.

THORKEL OF HERJOLFSNESS, a farmer in Greenland; shelters Thorbjorn Vifilsson and crew, *Eir*, 3; entertains the sybil Thorbjorg, *Eir*, 4.

THORLAK RUNOLFSSON, bishop of Skalholt 1118–33; descendant of Karlsefni, *Grl*, 9; *Eir*, 14.

THORSTEIN EIRIKSSON, son of Eirik the Red, *Grl*, 2, *Eir*, 5; marries Gudrid, *Grl*, 6, *Eir*, 6; sails for Vinland, reaches Lysufjord in Greenland, dies there, predicts Gudrid's future, *Grl*, 6; sails for Vinland with his father, returns to Greenland, *Eir*, 5; settles at Lysufjord with Gudrid, dies there, predicts her future, *Eir*, 6.

THORSTEIN THE BLACK, farmer at Lysufjord (called The Black only in *Grl*); shelters Thorstein Eiriksson and Gudrid, *Grl*, 6; owns Lysufjord jointly with Thorstein Eiriksson, is host to him and Gudrid, *Eir*, 6; helps Gudrid when she is widowed, moves to Eiriksfjord, *Grl*, 6.

THORSTEIN THE RED, a warrior king, son of Olaf the White and Aud the Deep-Minded; killed in Scotland, *Eir*, 1.

THORUNN, descendant of Karlsefni and mother of Bishop Bjorn, *Grl*, 9, *Eir*, 14.

THORUNN, mother of Karlsefni, *Eir*, 7; refuses to share house with Gudrid, is reconciled, *Eir*, 14.

THORVALD ASVALDSSON, father of Eirik the Red; leaves Norway, settles at Drangar in Iceland, dies there, *Grl*, 1, *Eir*, 2.

THORVALD EIRIKSSON, son of Eirik the Red, *Grl*, 2, *Eir*, 8 (footnote – H only); leads an expedition to Vinland, stays at Leif's Houses, names Kjalarness, is killed by Skrælings, *Grl*, 4,

5; goes to Vinland with Karlsefni, *Eir*, 8; is killed by a Uniped, *Eir*, 12.

THORVALD KODRANSSON, a missionary, forced to flee from Iceland, *Grl*, 1.

THORVARD OF GARDAR, a farmer in Greenland; marries Freydis, *Grl*, 2, *Eir*, 8; joins Karlsefni's expedition to Vinland, *Eir*, 8; joins Freydis' expedition to Vinland, is goaded by her into massacring Finnbogi and Helgi and their crew, *Grl*, 8.

THURID, daughter of Eyvind the Easterner, marries Thorstein the Red, *Eir*, 1.

TYRKIR THE SOUTHERNER, a German, Leif's foster-father; accompanies Leif to Vinland, *Grl*, 3; finds wild grapes, *Grl*, 4.

ULF CROW, father of Gunnbjorn Ulfsson, *Grl*, 1, *Eir*, 2.

VÆTILD, mother of the captured Skræling children, *Eir*, 12.

VALDIDIDA, a Skræling king, *Eir*, 12.

VALTHJOF OF VALTHJOFSTEAD; his farm destroyed by Eirik's slaves, *Eir*, 2.

VIFIL OF VIFILSDALE, a war captive, freed by Aud the Deep-Minded; grandfather of Gudrid, *Eir*, 1.

YNGVILD, descendant of Karlsefni and mother of Bishop Brand, *Grl*, 9, *Eir*, 14.

PLACE NAMES

ALPTAFJORD (now Sermilik), Helgi Thorbrandsson's land-claim in the Eastern Settlement of Greenland, *Grl*, 1.

ARNLAUGSFJORD, one of the original land-claims in the Eastern Settlement of Greenland, *Grl*, 1.

BJARN ISLES (or BJARN ISLE), Karlsefni's first landfall on his way to Vinland, somewhere off the west coast of Greenland, *Eir*, 8. Perhaps some unidentifiable cluster of islets off the east coast of Baffin Island; or if BJARN ISLE (the reading in H) is right, probably Disco Island, off Greenland.

BJARN ISLE ('Bear Isle'), island named by Karlsefni, somewhere to the south-east off the coast of Markland, *Eir*, 8.

BLASERK ('Blue-Shirt'), a glacier peak on the east coast of Greenland, in the region of Angmagssalik (probably Ingolfsfjeld), the first landmark sighted by Eirik, *Grl*, 1, *Eir*, 2.

BRATTAHLID (now Kagssiarssuk), Eirik's farm in Eiriksfjord, in the Eastern Settlement of Greenland, *Grl, Eir, passim.*

EASTERN SETTLEMENT, the more southerly of the two Icelandic settlements on the west coast of Greenland, in the present Julianehaab area, *Eir,* 1; see also Introduction, p. 18.

EINARSFJORD (now Igaliko), one of the original land-claims in the Eastern Settlement of Greenland, *Grl,* 1.

EIRIKSFJORD (now Tunugdliarfik), Eirik's home fjord, in the Eastern Settlement of Greenland, *Grl, Eir, passim.*

EIRIKS HOLMS, islands somewhere off the Eastern Settlement of Greenland, near Cape Farewell, where Eirik spent his second winter on Greenland, *Grl,* 1, *Eir,* 2.

EIRIKS ISLAND (now Igdlotalik), an island off the mouth of Eiriksfjord, where Eirik spent his first and third winters on Greenland, *Grl,* 1, *Eir,* 2.

FURDUSTRANDS ('Marvel Strands'), a long stretch of sandy coast named by Karlsefni, somewhere to the south of Markland, *Eir,* 8, 9. Possibly in the Gulf of St Lawrence, or on the coasts of Nova Scotia or New England.

GARDAR (now Igaliko), the farm in Einarsfjord where Freydis and Thorvard lived, *Grl,* 2, 8; later the residence of the Bishops of Greenland, *Grl,* 2.

GREENLAND, first named by Eirik, *Grl,* 1, *Eir,* 2, and *passim;* see also Introduction, pp. 16–23.

GREENLAND SEA (now Denmark Strait), the sea between Greenland and Iceland, *Grl,* 2, *Eir,* 13.

GUNNBJARNAR SKERRIES, a group of islets sighted by Gunnbjorn Ulfsson somewhere west of Iceland, *Grl,* 1, *Eir,* 2. Probably the islands to the east or north-east of Angmagssalik, in Greenland, see also Introduction, p. 16.

HAFGRIMSFJORD (now Ekaluit), a little fjord that branches off Einarsfjord, and one of the original land-claims in the Eastern Settlement of Greenland, *Grl,* 1.

HELLULAND ('Slab-Land'), Bjarni Herjolfsson's last landfall on his way back to Greenland from his accidental sighting of America, a glaciated rock-bound country, and Leif's first landfall on his way to find Bjarni's countries, and named by Leif, *Grl,* 3; a country covered with huge slabs of rock and named by Karlsefni on his way to Vinland, *Eir*, 8. It can only be the south-east coast of Baffin Island or some northerly part of the coast of Labrador.

HERJOLFSFJORD (now Amitsuarssuk), Herjolf Bardarson's land-claim in the Eastern Settlement of Greenland, *Grl*, 1.

HERJOLFSNESS (now Ikigait), Herjolf Bardarson's farm in Herjolfsness, inherited by Bjarni Herjolfsson, *Grl*, 1, 2; farm owned by Thorkel, who sheltered Thorbjorn Vifilsson, *Eir*, 3, 4.

HOPE ('Tidal Lake'), the area in Vinland where Karlsefni tried to establish a permanent settlement, *Eir*, 10, 11. Believed to be somewhere in New England, probably well to the south.

HRAFNSFJORD (now Agdluitsok), one of the original land-claims in the Eastern Settlement of Greenland, *Grl*, 1; explored by Eirik, *Grl*, 1, *Eir*, 2.

HVARFS PEAK (now Cape Farewell), a mountain on the southern tip of Greenland, *Grl*, 1, *Eir*, 2.

HVÍTRAMANNALAND ('White Men's Land'), a fabulous country said to lie opposite Vinland, *Eir*, 12.

KETILSFJORD (now Tasermiut), one of the original land-claims in the Eastern Settlement of Greenland, *Grl*, 1.

KJALARNESS ('Keelness'), a promontory somewhere north-east of Vinland, where Thorvald Eiriksson's ship was damaged and where the shattered keel was erected as a monument, *Grl*, 5; a promontory somewhere in Furdustrands where Karlsefni found a ship's keel and named the headland after it, *Eir*, 8, 9, 11.

KROSSANESS ('Cross-Ness'), the headland where Thorvald Eiriksson wanted to make his home, near Vinland, and where he was buried after being killed by Skrælings, *Grl*, 5.

LEIF'S HOUSES, the houses built by Leif Eiriksson in Vinland to winter in, and later lent to other explorers, *Grl*, 5, 7, 8.

LYSUFJORD (now Ameragdla), the farm in the Western Settlement of Greenland where Thorstein Eiriksson died, *Grl*, 6, *Eir*, 6.

MARKLAND ('Forest-Land'), a heavily-wooded country between Helluland and Vinland, named by Leif Eiriksson on his voyage of exploration, *Grl*, 3; named by Karlsefni in his colonizing expedition, *Eir*, 8; two Skræling children captured there by Karlsefni on his way back to Greenland, *Eir*, 12. Probably the south-east coast of Labrador, or Newfoundland.

MID GLACIER, Eirik's name for the glacier Blaserk, *Grl*, 1.

SIGLUFJORD (now Unartok, or the fjord to the north called Agdluitsok), one of the original land-claims in the Eastern Settlement of Greenland, *Grl*, 1.

SNÆFELL: a glacier on the west coast of Greenland, explored by Eirik, *Grl*, 1, *Eir*, 2.

SOLVADALE, one of the original land-claims in the Eastern Settlement of Greenland, at the head of the fjord now called Kangikitsok, *Grl*, 1.

STOKKANESS (now Kiagtukt), Thorbjorn Vifilsson's home in the Eastern Settlement of Greenland, *Eir*, 4.

STRAUM ISLAND ('Current Island'), an island in the mouth of Straumfjord, where Karlsefni spent his first winter on his Vinland expedition, *Eir*, 8.

STRAUMFJORD ('Current Fjord'), a fjord with fierce currents somewhere north of Vinland, where Karlsefni spent his first winter, *Eir*, 8; perhaps used as a base by the main party while Karlsefni explored to the south, *Eir*, 11, 12. Identifications have ranged from Long Island Sound in the south to various bays in the Gulf of St Lawrence.

THJODHILD'S CHURCH, the church built by Eirik's wife, near Brattahlid in Greenland, *Eir*, 5.

UNIPED-LAND: a fabulous country said to be near Vinland, where Thorvald Eiriksson was killed, *Eir*, 12.

VATNA DISTRICT ('Lake District'), one of the original land-claims in the Eastern Settlement of Greenland, between Siglufjord and Einarsfjord, *Grl*, 1.

VINLAND ('Wine-Land'), the country explored by Leif Eiriksson and named by him, *Grl*, 4; visited by Thorvald Eiriksson and explored further, *Grl*, 5; visited by Karlsefni and made the site of his attempted settlement, *Grl*, 7; visited by Freydis for a winter, *Grl*, 8; accidentally discovered by Leif Eiriksson, *Eir*, 5; sought by Karlsefni as a site for a permanent settlement, *Eir*, 8, 9, 10; called Vinland the Good, *Eir*, 8 (footnote).

Probably somewhere on the southern New England coast. See also Introduction, pp. 23–9.

WESTERN SETTLEMENT, the more northerly of the two Icelandic settlements on the west coast of Greenland, in the present Godthaab area, *Grl*, 1, 6, *Eir*, 6; Karlsefni's point of departure for Vinland, *Eir*, 8. See also Introduction, page 18.

CHRONOLOGICAL TABLE

Vikings sack Lindisfarne	A.D. 793
Vikings sack Iona and Lambay	795
Irish hermits in Iceland	c. 795
Iceland described by the Irish monk Dicuil	825
Norsemen discover Iceland	c. 860
Settlement of Iceland begins	c. 870
Gunnbjorn Ulfsson sights Greenland	c. 900
Icelandic republic established	930
Eirik the Red emigrates to Iceland	c. 960
Snæbjorn Galti's expedition to Greenland	c. 978
Eirik the Red explores Greenland	c. 981
Eirik the Red colonizes Greenland	985/6
Bjarni Herjolfsson sights America	985/6
Iceland adopts Christianity	1000
Leif Eiriksson explores Vinland	c. 1001
Thorfinn Karlsefni in Vinland	c. 1010
Iceland makes 'explorers' treaty' with Norway	c. 1022
Adam of Bremen writes about Vinland	c. 1075
Bishop Eirik seeks Vinland	1121
Greenland bishopric established	1126
Ari the Learned writes *Íslendingabók*	c. 1127
Spitzbergen discovered	before 1170
Grænlendinga Saga written	?c. 1190
Jan Mayen Island discovered	1194
Eirik's Saga written	?c. 1260
Greenland comes under Norwegian rule	1261
Iceland comes under Norwegian rule	1262
Hauksbók MS. compiled	c. 1330
Western Settlement in Greenland wiped out	c. 1345
Markland (Labrador) visited by Greenlanders	1347
Flateyjarbók MS. compiled	c. 1390
Last ship from Greenland reaches Iceland	1410
Skálholtsbók MS. compiled	c. 1470
Papal letter on Greenland	1492
Christopher Columbus rediscovers America	1492
Norse colony in Greenland dies out	c. 1500

This map was drawn in Iceland by Sigurdur Stefansson, *circa* 1590, showing the northern Atlantic, with Great Britain and Norway to the east, the Arctic Ocean to the north, and Greenland, 'Helleland' (Baffin Island?), 'Markland' (Labrador?), 'Skrælinge Land' (Land of the Skrælings – Native American Land), and 'Promontorium Winlandiæ' (Vinland Promontory) to the west.

Stefansson appended the following explanatory notes to his map. Below them is a rough translation.

A. Hi sunt, ad quos Angli pervenerunt, ab ariditate nomen habent tanquem vel solis, vel frigoris adustione torridi et exsiccati.

B. His proxime est Vinlandia, quam propter terrae, faecunditatem et utilium rerum uberem proventum, Bonam dixere. Hanc a meridie oceanum finire voluere nostri. Sed ego ex recentiorum historiis colligo, aut fretum aut sinum hanc ab America distinguere.

A [Skrælinge Land]. These people, whom the English reached, get their name from their aridity; they are dried up just as much by the heat as the cold.

B [Promontorium Winlandiae]. Next to them lies Vinland, which is called The Good because of the fertility of the land and its abundant produce of useful things. Our historians have wanted to make the ocean its southern boundary, but from more recent accounts I deduce that it is separated from America either by a strait or a bay.

Map 1. North Atlantic map drawn by Sigurdur Stefansson
in Iceland, c. 1590

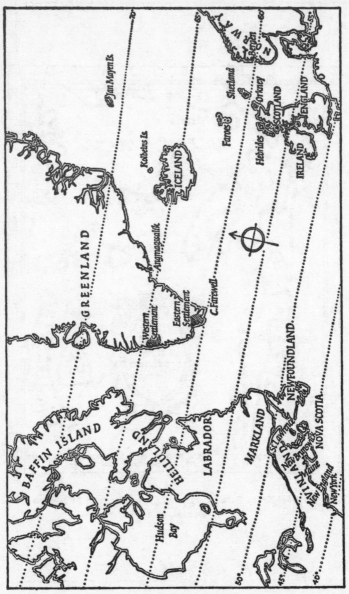

Map 2. The Atlantic

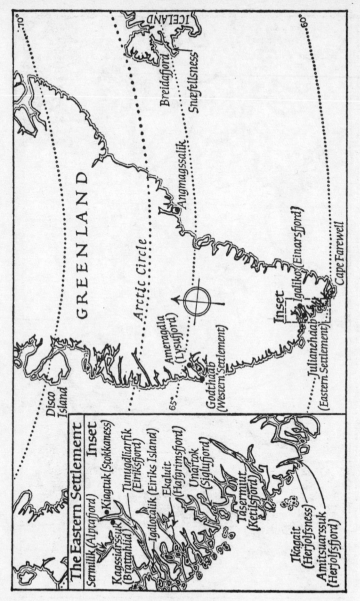

Map 3. Greenland

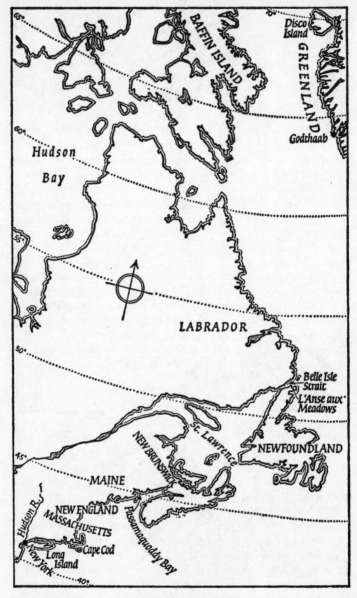

Map 4. North America

POSTSCRIPT
In memoriam Hermann Pálsson

Some intriguing developments in the Vinland story have occurred since the original publication. A great deal of research into the climatic history of the north has been carried out, offering a detailed picture of the weather conditions which the Norse explorers would have met and clarifying the last decades of the doomed Norse colonies in Greenland. The archaeological investigations which were going on at L'Anse aux Meadows in Newfoundland in the 1960s have been corroborated by further excavations, and the site is now a key landmark on the tourist map of Canada. Several books have been published containing new theories about the location of Vinland, such as *The Wineland Millennium: Saga and Evidence* by Páll Bergþórsson (Reykjavik, 2000) and *Vikings: the North Atlantic Saga*, ed. William W. Fitzhugh and Elisabeth I. Ward (Smithsonian Institute Press, 2000).

Perhaps the most spectacular event since the first appearance of our translation was the purchase by Yale University, and subsequent publication in 1965, of the so-called 'Vinland Map', which was claimed to be an authentic Norse map of the world dating from around 1440 and purporting to delineate the 'Vinland' discovered by the Norsemen. It was initially hailed with considerable enthusiasm by many (including myself!) as clinching evidence to confirm the accuracy of the saga traditions about Vinland; but it did nothing of the sort. Serious scholars of cartography and Norse studies were deeply sceptical about the map and its provenance from the outset, and suspected that it might be a modern forgery. But who forged it, and when, and why? After many years of controversy and bitter dispute, the mystery has now been solved by the Norwegian-born scholar Kirsten A. Seaver (*Maps, Myths, and Men: the Story of the Vinland Map* (Stanford University Press, 2004)). She has proved beyond any reasonable doubt that the map was forged in Austria shortly before the Second World War by a Jesuit cartographic historian Father Joseph Fischer (1858–1944), who was creating the map he had always believed *must* have existed; after the War it surfaced, like so many other lost or stolen artifacts, on the antiquarian market and was sold to Yale University through a complicated and ingenious scam.

More importantly, from a personal point of view, this edition allows me to pay tribute to my friend, collaborator and mentor Hermann Pálsson (1921–2002), Professor Emeritus of Icelandic Studies at the

University of Edinburgh, who died after an accident in Bulgaria. He was one of the most eminent and erudite Icelandic scholars of his generation, and did an enormous amount to illuminate the Icelandic Sagas for the English-speaking world.

Hermann was born on a farm in the north of Iceland, the sixth child in a family of twelve. He earned a degree in Icelandic studies at the University of Iceland (1943–7), and an honours degree in Celtic studies at the University College, Dublin in 1950, which gave him a significant insight into Irish influences on Norse literature which few specialists in Icelandic could boast at the time. As a young lecturer at Edinburgh University in the 1950s he created a centre of excellence for Norse studies which became a magnet for students and the envy of many other institutions.

His speciality was the medieval literature of Iceland and its relationship with European humanism. He published several books in which he explored this fertile field: he showed that the sagas were not a uniquely indigenous flowering of native genius sprouting from the virgin soil of Iceland, but had benefited immensely from influences from abroad – not just from Ireland but also from mainstream European thinking and literature. He published studies on many of the major prose sagas and Eddaic poems, as well as several books and articles on the origins and context of saga writing (and reading) in medieval Iceland, for which he coined the term *sagnaskemmtun* ('saga entertainment').

For my own part, I would mention his huge contribution to introducing the Icelandic sagas to the English-speaking world with a series of ground-breaking translations, including his help with my first translation, *Njal's Saga* (Penguin Classics 1960). (Others are given in the biographical note at the front of this volume.)

On one of the last occasions we were together, we found that our thoughts on the Vinland Sagas had been coalescing: we had come to believe that 'Vinland' had never existed as a precise geographical location in North America. The name itself – 'Vinland the Good' – carries too many overtones of romance and fable: fables of the Hesperides, of the Fortunate Isles (*Insulae Fortunatae*), of *Hvítramannaland* (The Land of the White People'), of the Irish *Immrama* (Voyages) in their Lives of Saints. '*Vinland the Good*' smacks much more of a wistful and wishful concept than of a geographical reality. To the Norse explorers, Vinland was always somewhere beyond the next horizon – tantalizingly near, but always just out of reach.

Magnus Magnusson
November, 2003